Off Off Broadway Festival Plays

Thirty-Fifth Series

WHITE EMBERS
by Saviana Stanescu

SKIN DEEP
by Mary Lynn Dobson

PIGSKIN
by Gabriel Jason Dean

DANCE LESSONS
by Josh Koenigsberg

THE MUD IS THICKER IN MISSISSIPPI
by Dennis A. Allen II

THE BEAR (A Tragedy)
by E.J.C. Calvert

A SAMUEL FRENCH ACTING EDITION

SAMUEL FRENCH

FOUNDED 1830

NEW YORK HOLLYWOOD LONDON TORONTO

SAMUELFRENCH.COM

MUSIC USE NOTE

Licensees are solely responsible for obtaining formal written permission from copyright owners to use copyrighted music in the performance of this play and are strongly cautioned to do so. If no such permission is obtained by the licensee, then the licensee must use only original music that the licensee owns and controls. Licensees are solely responsible and liable for all music clearances and shall indemnify the copyright owners of the play and their licensing agent, Samuel French, Inc., against any costs, expenses, losses and liabilities arising from the use of music by licensees.

IMPORTANT BILLING AND CREDIT REQUIREMENTS

All producers of *WHITE EMBERS, SKIN DEEP, PIGSKIN, DANCE LESSONS, THE MUD IS THICKER IN MISSISSIPPI,* and *THE BEAR (A TRAGEDY)* must give credit to the Authors of the Play in all programs distributed in connection with performances of the Play, and in all instances in which the title of the Play appears for the purposes of advertising, publicizing or otherwise exploiting the Play and/or a production. The name of the Authors *must* appear on a separate line on which no other name appears, immediately following the title and *must* appear in size of type not less than fifty percent of the size of the title type.

35th Annual

SAMUEL FRENCH
Off Off Broadway Short Play Festival
July 13th-18th

The Lion Theatre
Theatre Row
NYC

Dear Friends,

We are very proud to say that the 2010 Samuel French Off Off Broadway Short Play Festival brought the largest submission response we've ever seen! Nearly 900 entries were received, from across the country and internationally. This, by far, is the largest number of submissions in the Festival's 35 year history.

This increase speaks volumes, not only about the number of motivated playwrights in our industry, but also their determination to be heard among a symphony of talented voices. We hope our Festival is driving playwrights to dig deeper, take more risks, and cultivate the courage to express themselves without hesitation.

Of course, as competition is an integral part of this Festival, hard decisions had to be made. After countless rounds of script reading, careful evaluation, and an outstanding week of performances, we've compiled the six winners presented in this collection.

This gifted group of playwrights represents a very special body of work. These plays are challenging, honest, and, we hope, inspirational. They represent a range of writers, some just beginning their career in the theatre, and some who are internationally recognized for their work. However, all are, in different ways, "emerging," and we are incredibly grateful that they have shared their talent with us.

We'd also like to express our gratitude toward our illustrious 2010 panel of Festival judges for their time and expertise in guiding this process. The 18 judges–comprised of professional playwrights, agents, and Artistic Directors from some of our nation's boldest theatres–were instrumental throughout the performance week as the six winners were selected.

Finally, we'd like to thank you, the reader, for recognizing and supporting new play development. By reading these plays (and hopefully, producing them on your stages) you are lending your support to these deserving playwrights and to the future of playwriting. We would also like to encourage you to check out our other volumes of Festival winners as we have accumulated a wonderful and varied selection of short plays over the past 35 years.

It is my honor on behalf of the Samuel French Board of Directors, the Festival Staff, and all the employees in our New York, Los Angeles and London offices, to present to you to the winners of the 35th Annual Samuel French Off Off Broadway Short Play Festival.

Sincerely,

Kenneth Dingledine
Festival Coordinator

The Samuel French Off Off Broadway Short Play Festival started in 1975 and is one of the nation's most established and highly regarded short play festivals. During the course of the Festival's first 34 years, over 500 theatre companies and schools participated in the Festival, including companies from coast to coast as well as abroad from Canada, Singapore, and the United Kingdom. Over the years, 194 submitted plays have been published, with many of the participants becoming established, award-winning playwrights.

Festival Coordinator: Kenneth Dingledine
Production Coordinator: Billie Davis
Literary Coordinator: Roxane Heinze-Bradshaw
Assistant Literary Coordinator: Katy DiSavino
Online Content Director/Interview Series Editor: Amy Rose Marsh
Press/Public Relations: Ron Lasko
Graphic Design: Gene Sweeney
Lighting Design: Miriam Crowe
Judge Liaison: Katie Henry
Board Operator: Casey McLain

Festival Crew: Matthew Ackers, Jordan Barsky, Amy Cruz, Lauren Espenhart, Melody Frenandez, Joe Ferreira, Jake Glickman, Sarah Karpati, Matthew Klein, Maura Krause, Ashley Kuske, Josephine Messina, Sara Mirowski, José Munoz, Dora Naughton, Richard Patterson, Megan Strub, Robin Sandusky

SAMUEL FRENCH STAFF

Samuel French President & C.E.O.: Leon Embry
Samuel French Vice-President: Abbie Van Nostrand
Director of Operations: Gwen Feldman
Director of Finance: Rita Maté
Director of Professional Licensing: Brad Lohrenz
Director of Amateur Licensing: Melody Fernandez
Director of Licensing Operations: Lori Thimsen
Contracts Manager: Lysna Marzani

GUEST JUDGES

David Adjmi	Frances Hill	Carmen Rivera
Jim Brochu	Tina Howe	Joseph Rosswog
Jason Egan	Morgan Jenness	David Saint
Scott Edwards	Deborah Laufer	Buddy Thomas
Corinne Hayoun	Craig Lucas	Jeff Zinn
	Antje Oegel	

CONTENTS

WHITE EMBERS

A pseudo-thriller

by Saviana Stanescu

WHITE EMBERS was produced by Christopher Mirto at the Lion Theatre at Theatre Row), on July 14th, 2010. The performance was directed by Christopher Mirto, with dramaturgy by Anne Seiwerath. The cast was as follows:

ALEX	Jason Martin
VICKI	Martyna Majok
SHARI	Laura Gragtmans
LESLIE	Lisa Kitchens

CHARACTERS

SHARI – early 30s
VICKY – late 20s
ALEX – 30s-40s
LESLIE – 30s-40s

TIME

present

PLACE

Connecticut, USA

ABOUT THE AUTHOR

Saviana Stanescu (www.saviana.com) is a renowned Romanian-born writer based in New York City. Her plays have been widely presented internationally and in the US. Recent New York productions include *Aliens With Extraordinary Skills* (The Women's Project, published by Samuel French), *Waxing West* (2007 New York Innovative Theatre Award for Outstanding Full-length Script), and *YokastaS Redux* at La MaMa Theatre, *Flag Stories* at TBG Theatre (part of Myth America Project, a collage of texts by Arthur Kopit, Theresa Rebeck, Israel Horowitz, Jason Grote, etc.), *Suspendida and Vicious Dogs on Premises* (with Witness Relocation) at the Ontological Theatre, *Balkan Blues* at the NYC Fringe Festival, *the E-Dating Project* at Strasberg Institute for Theatre & Film, and the site-specific *I want what you have* at the World Financial Center. Saviana's plays have received readings and workshops at Long Wharf Theatre, New York Theatre Workshop, The Lark, New York Stage & Film, Baryshnikov Arts Center, Playwrights' Foundation, Traveling Jewish Theatre, Immigrants Theatre Project, LaGuardia Performing Arts Center, Origin Theatre Company, etc.

She has published books of poetry and drama including *Aliens With Extraordinary Skills, Waxing West, Google me!* (poetry), *Black Milk* (four plays) and *The Inflatable Apocalypse* (Best Romanian Play of the Year UNITER Award in 2000). Other published work includes: monologues and scenes in Smith & Kraus annual anthologies, *Aurolac Blues,* performed at HERE Arts Center, in the anthology *Plays and Playwrights 2006*; two monologues in the Playwrights' Center's *Monologues for Women, Jelly-Love and Peanut-Butter* in the "Estrogenius" anthology of new plays by women.

Saviana was a 2005-2007 TCG fellow with the Lark Play Development Center, where her plays *Waxing West* and *Lenin's Shoe* had barebones productions. She is currently leading the Eastern European Exchange Program for the Lark. She was a 2007-2008 NYSCA playwright-in-residence with Women's Project and writer-in-residence for Richard Schechner's East Coast Artists. She holds an MA in Performance Studies (Fulbright fellow) and an MFA in Dramatic Writing (John Golden Award for excellence in playwriting) from New York University, Tisch School of the Arts, where she now teaches in the Drama Department.

(The set is composed only of various chairs. Among them a white one.)

(Right-stage: Two women on the roof of a house. **VICKY** *wears a home gown,* **SHARI** *wears jeans and has a gun in her right hand. She has a heavy accent. Although she points the gun at* **VICKY***, she seems more interested in admiring the view.)*

(Left-stage: **LESLIE** *and* **ALEX** *on a plane. [There's no need for a realistic set, two chairs and fastened belts would do it.])*

(Lights up on **SHARI** *and* **VICKY***.)*

SHARI.	VICKY.
The roof of the new world…	
It's beautiful…	It's freezing…

SHARI. Closer to the sky…

VICKY. My feet are turning red…

SHARI. Sky-scraping…Sky-skiing…

VICKY. I'm getting frostbite. My feet are turning purple.

SHARI. Oh. *(looking at* **VICKY***'s feet)* Your funny little toes… *(chanting and 'conducting' with the gun)* Little worms in the snow on the roof…

VICKY. Careful! …Listen to me, Telma. You are a sensitive person. A nice woman. You don't want to kill me. You're not a criminal.

SHARI. My name is not Telma.

VICKY. *(impatiently)* Is not Telma?! Who are you then? Where is Telma Khan?

SHARI. Oh, yes. You invited Telma Khan for a – how did you call it? – "chat" on Bechnian cuisine.

VICKY. What did you do to Telma?

SHARI. I killed her. *(beat)* Relax. I was Telma Khan just for you. For a while. I took the name from that movie "Telma and Louise." I liked that movie.

VICKY. Are you gonna take me on a road trip?

SHARI. Maybe. Relax now.

VICKY. How can I relax when you're pointing a gun at me? When I'm FREEZING.

SHARI. Have you ever watched the sky from the top roof of your house?

VICKY. What are you planning to do with me? Do you wanna kill me? No, you can't kill me. That would be a big mistake. A sin. It would be silly. Crazy. It can get you…deported! Or worse. There is death penalty in this country!

SHARI. Relax. Enjoy the view. Feel the snow.

VICKY. I haven't done anything to you.

SHARI. Look up at the sky! The sun. The eye. Of God.

VICKY. Yeah, God is there, up there. He's looking at us. Almighty God is looking at you. Let's…pray! Pray with me! Thank you God for such a beautiful night, life is good and beautiful, we thank you, God, for our humble life, thank you for this world and this life / and…

SHARI. Shut up! There are no Gods here, just the snow… It's a warm snow here in America…Goodbye, snow. Say, goodbye, to the snow! Adala, zaka! Adala!

*(Lights up on **LESLIE** and **ALEX**.)*

LESLIE. I'm nervous.

ALEX. Relax. It's not your first time on a plane.

LESLIE. It's not the plane. It's…a headache. I've got this awful headache.

ALEX. I told you to drink tea not coffee.

LESLIE. It's not the coffee… It's… What if…what if she's… I don't know…different.

ALEX. Everyone is different.

LESLIE. Yes, but…there's different and 'different'…

ALEX. *(trying to get some sleep)* We'll see. There's no need to think of this now.

LESLIE. Yes, but…we can't go there and not take her, can we?

ALEX. I suppose we can.

LESLIE. No, pumpkin, we can't play with those kids' lives. It's enough that they live in a third world country!

ALEX. Try to get some sleep, pumpkin. Or read your book.

LESLIE. I finished that one on the history of Bechnya. Sad, very sad, country. Ethnic conflicts, wars, invasions… I've been saying this to everyone since Vietnam: Make Love, not War! War is stupid! War is / brainwashing. It's…

ALEX. Shhhhh! People want to sleep on the plane. It's a long trip.

LESLIE. I can't sleep. And I don't have anything to read.

ALEX. The English-Bechnyan travel guide.

(Lights shift on **VICKY** *and* **SHARI.** **SHARI** *is taking her shoes off with her left hand. The gun in her right hand is still pointed at* **VICKY.** *)*

VICKY. Say something for God's sake! *(beat)* What's all this about? What do you want? You want money? We can go inside and I'll write you a neat check…

SHARI. Feel the snow with your bare feet… Do you hear anything? The snow tells you a story…listen to it!

VICKY. Oh, yes…sure… The snow tells me a story. A fairy-tale.

SHARI. Shhhhhh!

VICKY. The snow says we should go inside. She…the snow… will speak to me through the…window.

SHARI. You don't think I can hurt you. I can hurt you. *(pointing the gun at her)* Walk! Walk in front of me. Walk!

*(***VICKY*** walks, ***SHARI*** walks on her foot steps.)*

Feel the snow, feel it! It's hot. Good. Tender. It's walking on white embers…

VICKY. It's pneumonia. We'll both get pneumonia. Do you know what pneumonia means?

SHARI. Maybe we see the sky and the snow for the last time. Look at the sky, feel the snow, taste the air, take the memory of them with you. Pneumonia means nothing… *(She pushes* **VICKY**.*)* OK, you want to go inside, let's go inside! We'll finish our conversation very quickly inside.

VICKY. *(changing her strategy)* Wait. Look! See that bird on the sky…

SHARI. Where?

VICKY. There.

SHARI. I don't see it.

VICKY. How do you say bird in Bechnyan?

SHARI. Kaneper.

VICKY. Snow?

SHARI. Zaka. I don't see the bird.

VICKY. Sky?

SHARI. Kari.

(As **SHARI** *looks up at the sky,* **VICKY** *attempts to snatch her gun. They start fighting for the gun in the snow.)*

VICKY. *(on top of* **SHARI***)* Fucking bitch! Fucking crazy bitch!

SHARI. *(on top of* **VICKY***)* Fakiti moka, adala moka!

(Lights shift on **LESLIE** *and* **ALEX**.*)*

LESLIE. "Adala" – good bye. Adala! With an accent on the first syllable. Adala! "Ada" – water. My arms still hurt from carrying that damn bag. 25 bottles of water! That's silly to carry ordinary water over there…

ALEX. You'll ask for it when you need to brush your teeth.

LESLIE. It's offensive to them. You know that woman Fahida who works for the Taylors. I asked her if they had hot water at home and she got all stiff: "What do you think, we're barbarians, of course we had hot water: Tuesday and Saturday from 6-8 pm. Plenty of hot water! And we had bathtubs, too…AND public baths!" Bechnyans care about their pride.

ALEX. I hope we can buy a few more bottles at the airport.

LESLIE. That's ridiculous…

ALEX. You got chocolate and teddy-bears…

LESLIE. For the girl not for me…Jesus!

(Lights shift.)

(Living Room)

*(**VICKY** is sitting in a chair, **SHARI** ties her hands to the back of the chair.)*

VICKY. It hurts.

SHARI. It will make you stay quiet – how did you call me? – bitch! We are going to have a nice "chat," bitch.

*(**SHARI** looks around the house.)*

You have a fancy house. Modern. Very modern. *(starts inspecting the room)* Who decorated it?

*(**VICKY** doesn't want to answer. **SHARI** points the gun at **VICKY**'s head.)*

Speak!

VICKY. James. My husband. He's an architect.

SHARI. I've never seen white chairs. Ours are brown, gray or black over there.

VICKY. You only need some white paint and they can be white.

SHARI. A naked woman in a white chair looks…white.

VICKY. Oh, no. You won't have me sitting naked in that chair.

SHARI. You'd look beautiful. Snow-white. Zaka-alba.

VICKY. You have a crush on me? That's it? You want…me?

SHARI. *(Touching **VICKY**'s upper body with the gun, she notices the label Victoria's Secret.)* "Victoria's Secret." What's your secret, Victoria? Tell me your secret.

VICKY. Leave me alone…

*(Lights up on **LESLIE** and **ALEX** in a waiting room.)*

LESLIE. It's cold…

ALEX. Freezing... I told you to take two sweaters.

LESLIE. Those kids live in this temperature on a daily basis, Alex, and you can't take it for a few minutes?

ALEX. Minutes? It's been more than an hour...this is unacceptable...we are foreigners, guests, we should be treated with some decency, respect, something... That gloomy woman with a bird-face is not happy to have us here... She looks like a raven, did you notice that?

LESLIE. Shut up, pumpkin. Would you like someone saying you look like a...parrot?

(Lights shift.)

SHARI. *(looking at a framed photo)* So this is your man... You deserve better... He's fat. Self-sufficient. Rich... happy...

VICKY. I don't know about happy...

SHARI. And these are your kids...

VICKY. Emma and Michael. Emma is eight, Michael is four.

SHARI. Your daughter is pretty... She looks like you.

VICKY. She has James's mouth...

SHARI. No, she doesn't.

VICKY. *(trying another strategy)* They're at school now. I should go fetch them home, shouldn't I?... You must tell Emma that you think she's pretty. Since she got those braces we've had only problems. She keeps saying she's ugly and that's why nobody loves her.

SHARI. She's not ugly.

VICKY. Exactly. James made fun of her once. He went like, "Where's my precious ugly girl?" She took it seriously. We had tears, screams, hunger strikes...the whole arsenal of misery... *(beat)* Let me go get the kids home. You're not that cruel to let two poor kids wait for their mom. You might have children too, you know how it is...

SHARI. I don't.

(Lights shift.)

LESLIE. Why should they treat us special? It's our fault. We arrived one day earlier.

ALEX. It's still rude... We should complain to her supervisor...

LESLIE. She is the supervisor.

ALEX. Maybe they need time to prepare the girl...

LESLIE. What's to prepare? We want to see her unprepared. Herself. I don't want to meet some Barbie-girl smiling and reciting lines they inscribed onto her mind...

ALEX. Damn, it's so cold.

LESLIE. You should make an effort to look warmer. The first impression means a lot.

(Lights shift.)

SHARI. Liar. They're not at school, it's winter break. I'm not stupid. You sent them to your mother-in-law. You stayed at home to finish your book. The cook-book. How's that to write a cook-book?

VICKY. It's not a cook-book, it's a restaurant guide...

SHARI. I know. You're a fancy food critic. Isn't that a good job? You go out and eat, and they pay you to write how you liked the food. You have silly jobs here in America.

VICKY. You seem to know a lot about me.

SHARI. I did some research. Like you did. On me and Bechnyan cuisine. *(She starts laughing.)*

(Lights shift.)

ALEX. You shouldn't expect her to love us at first sight.

LESLIE. That's exactly what I expect. A deep connection. At the first sight. I loved her at the first sight.

ALEX. Of her photo... You should be prepared for... I don't know, the unexpected.

LESLIE. Why do you always have to pull me down, pumpkin?

ALEX. It's called reality. And the reality is: she's a little Muslim girl.

LESLIE. We already had this conversation: she's not Muslim, she's only two years old! We'll be raising her Christian.

(Lights shift.)

SHARI. You had a nice life, girl. A beautiful boring life…

VICKY. You can have a nice life, too. You're a pretty woman. You can have fun. You can date someone! You can marry a nice guy, have kids, go on vacations…

SHARI. *(sticking the gun in* **VICKY***'s mouth)* Don't try to sell me the American Dream pie! I'm not buying it anymore. Have no money for it. Have no time. What do you know about me? Nothing. Let me tell you something: I've been living in the shelter next to your church for the last three months. I was there every Sunday, starring at you. You don't remember me. You don't know me. But I know everything about you. And a lot about shelters. I'm an expert. I can write a book on shelters and orphanages. Nobody will buy it, of course.

(Lights shift.)

LESLIE. I'm sure we will connect. You'll see. She will love us. She's our daughter. I've been thinking intensely of her for the last six months. She must have felt something.

ALEX. I doubt it… She doesn't even know we exist.

LESLIE. Of course she does! You want to pick up a fight, pumpkin? Now? Now when we're about to change our lives. When we're about to be more than ourselves, more than Leslie and Alex: a family, a true family.

ALEX. There's no need to be overdramatic.

LESLIE. There's no need to pretend that nothing important is happening.

(Lights shift.)

*(***SHARI*** takes the gun out of* **VICKY***'s mouth.)*

VICKY. Listen. I know what you need: a nice warm friendly place. *(smiling)* Let me accommodate you here for a while. You'll like it here. We can cook, read, write, talk… Like two girlfriends…two colleagues…two sisters…

SHARI. Two sisters?... Aren't you a funny doll? The first thing you'll do is call the Police and get rid of me. I know what that smile on your face means. It means nothing. You Americans smile and laugh and mean nothing. You ask 'how're you doing' and when we answer, you're far away, you don't need an answer. 'Fine', 'good', that's what we have to say. But what if it's not good? What if it's bad?... I worked with Americans over there. They helped us "build a new democracy." From our rubble and their bombs. They taught us how to smile and mean nothing. They finally gave me a visa to come over here. I must have smiled pretty well...

(Lights shift.)

LESLIE. We should choose a name for her...

ALEX. She already has a name...

LESLIE. What about...Mary? No, Mary is too common.

VICKY. I understand your frustration. You had a difficult life. You grew bitter. I understand that. But you won't feel any better if you hurt other people. You won't feel better.

SHARI. *(slapping* VICKY*)* You don't understand shit.

VICKY. There's no need for violence...

SHARI. There's no need for masks. *(caressing her)* Beautiful face...too beautiful to be true. How much did it cost you? Hmm? How much does it cost to erase wrinkles, scares, memories?

VICKY. I didn't have a face lift, if that's what you mean...

SHARI. Liar. You know what I mean.

VICKY. I have no idea what you mean...

LESLIE. We must find something exotic but not too exotic...

ALEX. What about Cleopatra? Cleo.

LESLIE. No. It's a fish name.

ALEX. It's a queer's name! All right. Let's just wait in silence.

LESLIE. Well, maybe an exotic name is not such a good idea.

SHARI. Vicky is a stupid name.

VICKY. My hands must have turned red...

LESLIE. I can't wait in silence AND in cold.

SHARI. I am going to call you Fatma, what about that?

VICKY. Call me whatever you want, but please do something about this rope, it really hurts!

SHARI. A beautiful name Fatma.

VICKY. I can't feel my hands. Can you do something with this rope? Loose it a bit? I can't even think clearly anymore... What's all this about?! What the hell is all this about? Why are you here? What the fuck do you want from me?! What's going on, for God's sake?

(She starts crying.)

SHARI. Oh, no. Don't cry, Fatma, don't cry. I can't see you crying. I'm loosing the rope, I'm loosing it, don't cry! Shhhhhhh!

*(She loses the rope but keeps the gun pointed at **VICKY**.)*

You need a blanket. It's getting cold. Where is your bedroom?

VICKY. Upstairs. The first one on your left.

*(**SHARI** goes offstage. **VICKY** tries to untie her hands.)*

LESLIE. What about Sabrina? Flora?! Linda!

ALEX. Whores' names. Or transvestites'.

LESLIE. You are full of prejudices, you still are!

ALEX. Anyway, she has a name, she has a past. It's not like she's being born now.

LESLIE. What past are you talking about? Two years in this horrible place, with those gloomy women watching over her. Two years to be erased from her memory. When we get home, she'll have the pink room, she'll have the bears...

ALEX. 27 plush bears!

LESLIE. 28.

ALEX. Maybe she doesn't like teddy-bears. What if bears frighten her... What if she's allergic to plush?

LESLIE. *(rummaging in her bag, pulling out a teddy bear)* I don't know anyone who's allergic to plush. Jesus. Your goal is to scare me on this trip. Plush bears are cute. I bet she never had one. She's going to love them.

ALEX. We can't be sure.

LESLIE. *(She takes a photo out of the bag.)* She's so cute. You like teddy-bears, little pumpkin, don't you? Of course, you do. Everyone loves teddy-bears. You need to tell Mommy what you like and Mommy will get it for you. You're my precious little girl, my perfect little pumpkin. Nothing can stop us. You're my little victory... Oh, my God, I'm shivering. I found the perfect name: Victoria. VICKY!

*(**SHARI** gets back holding a blanket and a teddy-bear. She drops them on the floor. She points the gun at **VICKY**.)*

SHARI. My spoiled little lady and her teddy bears. She can't stay one hour tied in a chair, can she? She gets sad. She gets bored. She cries. I should tell her another funny story. About a six year-old girl who spent 64 hours tied to a chair. In the dark. In a cold empty room. In her own piss and shit. Talking with the rats and the cockroaches. Imploring them to be her friends.

*(She shows her feet to **VICKY**.)*

Didn't you notice? I miss three toes. No tooth-fairy for Shari but a 'toe-fairy' with a rat head. A rat-fairy. A little brown rat-fairy.

VICKY. God...

SHARI. You don't like my stories.

VICKY. But why? What happened? Who locked you in that room? You were only / a child...

SHARI. Why? Because Shari stole the supervisor's cake for her little pretty Fatma who was crying for a piece a cake. Did she give any bite to Shari? No, she didn't. She ate it all. But Shari was happy because Fatma was happy. Fatma was smiling.

*(She starts caressing **VICKY** with the gun.)*

VICKY. I'm not Fatma, Shari. I'm not. I am Vicky. I have a daughter myself. Her name is Emma. Emma, a pretty little girl like the one in your story. You don't want bad things to happen to pretty Emma's mom, do you, do you?

SHARI. Of course you're Fatma, Fatma.

(**ALEX** and **LESLIE** turn towards **VICKY** and **SHARI**.)

LESLIE. (to **VICKY**) Hi! …I'm Leslie, he is Alex. Leslie. Alex.

VICKY. (pointing at the snow out the window) Zaka! Zaka!

ALEX. What's your name, sweetie?

LESLIE. Don't ask her that! (to **VICKY**) Vicky. Say Vicky. My name is VICKY.

VICKY. Zaka!

SHARI. Fatma. Shari.

ALEX. She's the older one, Leslie. Look at her eyes. She's the girl in the picture. She had a hair-cut.

LESLIE. What are you talking about, Vicky is two years old and has long curly hair, here's / the photo…

ALEX. They must have sent us an old photo. They do such things here.

SHARI. Mama. Papa.

LESLIE. (to **SHARI**) Sweetie…there must be some mistake…

(**SHARI** takes a photo out of her pocket. It's a photo of **ALEX** and **LESLIE**.)

SHARI. Mama. Papa.

ALEX. She has our photo, Leslie, she's our girl.

SHARI. Shari, Fatma. Mama, Papa.

LESLIE. They didn't tell us she had a sister…

ALEX. We didn't ask…

LESLIE. Look at them. They're inseparable…

SHARI. Fatma. Shari.

LESLIE. Let's take both of them, pumpkin!

ALEX. We've got papers for ONE kid's adoption.

LESLIE. They should be happy we want to take two.

ALEX. We can take only one girl out of this country, pump-kin, whichever you want, but only one…

VICKY. *(smiling)* Zaka!

LESLIE. She's talking to us.

ALEX. She seems like a happy child.

LESLIE. Isn't that strange? And her ears are like yours, a little sharp…

ALEX. What do you mean?

LESLIE. I mean she looks a bit like you…

ALEX. She does, doesn't she?

LESLIE. Look, she has your smile! Your nice smile not the other one…

ALEX. She's so pretty and chubby…

LESLIE. The older one is dirty… Look at her neck!

ALEX. Well…Vicky is dirty, too…

LESLIE. Yes, but her skin is so…white…and, I don't know, luminous! Don't you think so?

ALEX. You wouldn't say she was born in this place…

LESLIE. Exactly!

ALEX. But this situation is…they put us in such a situation…

LESLIE. She's our daughter. She's Vicky. I can feel her.
    (smiling at **VICKY***)* What does Mommy have here?!

    (She hands the teddy-bear to **VICKY***, who takes it and smiles back.)*

    A teddy-bear! For Vicky!

SHARI. Fatma! *(pointing at herself)* SHARI!

ALEX. Yes, Shari. You're a brave girl. You take care of the little one. She's a cutie, isn't she?

    *(***ALEX*** tries to caress* **VICKY***,* **SHARI** *stops him.)*

ALEX. What's wrong, girl?! *(to* **LESLIE***, while smiling at* **SHARI***)* She scares me a bit.

LESLIE. Where's the curly hair she had in the photo… Did they use a wig or something? Just to make a good impression? I don't get it. Why to mislead us? Why to send an old photo of her?

ALEX. Maybe they don't take photos of the kids every year…

LESLIE. A bunch of crooks! Incompetents!

ALEX. I told you…

LESLIE. What are we going to do… It's awful…

ALEX. We can ask to see the other kids if you want.

LESLIE. And leave Vicky here? No way.

> (**SHARI** *grabs the teddy-bear from* **VICKY***'s hands and throws it away.*)

LESLIE. Hey, what are you doing?!

SHARI. Mama!

ALEX. It's going to be difficult. We must ask for some help.

LESLIE. *(to* **SHARI***)* You are a big girl. She is a small girl. She needs Mommy and Daddy. You are a big girl. You understand this. We will take your little sister to America. We will take good care of her. We love her. You love her, too. You must be happy for your sister.

ALEX. *(to* **SHARI***)* You will come to visit her, in America.

LESLIE. Don't lie to her…

ALEX. She doesn't understand English.

LESLIE. I don't want our daughter to hear you lying. *(to* **VICKY** *who's still smiling)* Yes, Vicky, pumpkin, smile to Mommy! Now smile to Daddy, too!

ALEX. Yes, sweetheart, give daddy your hand! Say hello to daddy, Vicky!

> (*They are giggling at* **VICKY***, ignoring* **SHARI***.*)

SHARI. Fatma! Fatma! *(pointing at the window)* Zaka, Fatma. Zaka!

> (**VICKY** *doesn't look at the window, she enjoys playing with the teddy-bear.* **SHARI** *starts hitting* **ALEX***'s chest with her fists and her feet.*)

ALEX. This is not good. You're a bad girl! A bad girl!

> (*Lights fade. Beat.*)

> (*Lights up on* **SHARI** *and* **VICKY** *in the living room.*)

SHARI. I am a bad girl, Fatma. I came here to kill you and set your house on fire.

VICKY. *(beat)* You don't have the heart to do this.

SHARI. I don't know about my heart.

(**SHARI** *starts taking off her clothes.*)

I'm Shari. My name is Shari. Shari. Shari. Shari.

VICKY. Shari. What are you doing?

SHARI. Stay still. I will let you go soon.

VICKY. Stop this, stop this, Shari!

SHARI. I am going to sit on white embers.

VICKY. Let me help you.

SHARI. You don't remember me…

(**SHARI** *kisses* **VICKY** *on her cheek and unties her.*)

It's OK… Why to remember, what's so good in remembering?

VICKY. Look. You can stay here with me. For however long you want.

SHARI. This is not my house.

VICKY. You can make it here in America. I can help you.

SHARI. It's too late.

VICKY. It's never too late.

SHARI. I love this American lie…

VICKY. You can be our…babysitter! Emma will love you! Even / Michael…

SHARI. I don't want to lie in front of children.

VICKY. There's no need to lie. You can be yourself, tell always the truth.

SHARI. Then I would have to teach them Bechnyan. Talk with them in Bechnyan.

VICKY. You speak very good English.

SHARI. I learned English only to speak to you.

VICKY. Then talk to me! Tell me about you. I want to know everything about you.

SHARI. My little liar…

(She continues stripping.)

VICKY. Please, put your clothes on. Please!

*(By now **SHARI** is [almost] naked. She points the gun at **VICKY**.)*

SHARI. Don't move!

*(**SHARI** sits in the white chair.)*

VICKY. Shari. Nothing is utterly bad and irreversible... This is not a horror movie... Put your clothes on! I'm going to cook a nice dinner for us...a five stars dinner!

SHARI. Come here and kneel down!

VICKY. SHARI...

*(**SHARI** shoots the teddy-bear.)*

No! Why are you doing this?

SHARI. Come here! ...Come!...

VICKY. What do you wanna do? You don't have to do this. Don't do this, Shari!

SHARI. *(pushing **VICKY** down)* Kiss my legs! Kiss them!

VICKY. No, Shari...

SHARI. Lick them! Lick my skin! Lick! Lick!

VICKY. You cannot ask / me to...

SHARI. *(pushing **VICKY** down)* Lick! Feel the taste! Lick!

*(**VICKY** starts licking **SHARI**'s calves. **SHARI** lifts the hand with the gun and looks at it. She touches her own body with the gun.)*

Go on! Lick!... Touch my legs, tie them with your tongue, bite me, bite me, little white rat-fairy...Yes ... Sister rat-fairy... Don't stop! Bite!... Yes... Yes... Taste me. Bite me. Remember me. Keep a piece of me with you, in you, Fatma... Don't leave me alone!... Leave me alone!... Snow-White has turned brown... She bites the poisoned apple... It tastes good, Fatma... Where are you, Fatma? Fatma?!

VICKY. I'm here, Shari, I'm here. Feel me. I'm here.

SHARI. Adala, Fatma... Adala!

VICKY. No! *(beat)* Kaneper! Kari! Zaka! Zaka! Zaka!

 *(**SHARI** caresses **VICKY** with the gun.)*

SHARI. Zaka, Fatma, zaka.

 (She raises the arm with the gun. Blackout.)

 (A gun shot.)

The End

SKIN DEEP

A Comedy

by Mary Lynn Dobson

SKIN DEEP was performed at the Porch Light Theatre, Glen Rock, New Jersey as part of their Spring Playwrights Festival, May 1, 2010. It was directed by Mary Lynn Dobson and the cast was as follows:

BRITTANY'S MOM...............................Syndi Szabo
AMBER'S MOM............................... Michelle Russell
CRISTAL'S MOM ....Ana Kalet
CAROLE MARIE DITTERMAN................... Catherine Rowe
ARLENE BECKER BASS.........................Terri Sturtevant
DONNA JANE BRUNELLI-PISSARELLO ....Jen Hanselman

SKIN DEEP was performed as part of the Shortened Attention Span One-Act Festival, June 17-20, 2010, at the Players Theatre, New York. It was produced by Peter Riga Jr., directed by Mary Lynn Dobson, and the production stage manager was Bob Dumpert. The cast was as follows:

BRITTANY'S MOM...............................Syndi Szabo
AMBER'S MOM............................... Michelle Russell
CRISTAL'S MOM ....Kirsten Rani Almeida
CAROLE MARIE DITTERMAN................... Catherine Rowe
ARLENE BECKER BASS.........................Terri Sturtevant
DONNA JANE BRUNELLI-PISSARELLO ....Jen Hanselman

The above cast, creative and production teams reprised their roles for The 35th Annual Samuel French Off Off Broadway Short Play Festival on July 14, 2010 at the Lions Theatre at Theatre Row, New York.

SKIN DEEP was named the winner of the Frostburg State University's One-Act Competition and was performed on September 24th and 25th, 2010 at the Palace Theatre in Frostburg, Maryland. It was produced by Gerry LaFemina, Frostburg State University's Center for Creative Writing and Front and Centre Stage Productions.

CHARACTERS

BRITTANY'S MOM: (25 to 32) Painfully plain, has zero self esteem and couldn't stand out in a crowd if she set her hair on fire. She was the girl who blended into the beige wall all her life. It wasn't so much she was picked-on, she was just forgotten – and at least when you're picked on, someone knows you're alive. Unlike the others, she is completely sincere and not a phony. She truly believes her daughter is the brightest, most wonderful light on earth and she cannot figure out for the life of her, why the world can't see it too.

AMBER'S MOM: (29 to 40) Housewife and stage/pageant mom. While she'll smile and pretend to be Cristal's Mom's friend, she really doesn't like her. She can't wait to give you her opinion and will, especially when it concerns someone else. She watches her daughter like a hawk so that she will never find herself in a mortifying situation like the famous one known as, "The Dreaded Pageant Cake Incident."

CRISTAL'S MOM: (29 to 40) Housewife and stage/pageant mom. While she'll smile and pretend to be Amber's Mom's friend, she really doesn't like her. One thing she enjoys flaunting at times is that she knows she has a slight advantage over everyone else because, while her daughter may not have beauty or talent, she has dogs.

CAROL MARIE DITTERMAN: (40 to 60) Pageant Coordinator and Director. Dressed in local store business wear ranging anywhere from Target to Chico's. She is the boss. She knows all the ins and outs of the pageantry world. She is pro at protecting her pageant, will say anything to justify it and is an expert at "deflecting."

ARLENE BECKER-BASS: (40 to 60) Pageant Coordinator and Judge. Dressed in the same ilk as Carol Marie. She is more the promoter and cheerleader. However, she will always follow Carol's lead, especially when it comes to "deflecting."

DONNA JANE BRUNELLI-PISARELLO: (36 to almost 50) Seasoned Beauty Queen who has been doing this for years and will continue to do this for years. She thinks it's all about her even when it's not. Because she knows every trick in the beauty pageantry book, she thinks that means she has an education. This is her life, this is her calling, this is her job. When she is 90, she will proudly wear the title of Miss Bladder Control if it means she gets a crown.

Each role can be individually cast or can be double cast:

BRITTANY'S MOM doubles as **DONNA JANE BRUNELLI-PISARELLO**, **AMBER'S MOM** and **CRYSTAL'S MOM** double as the Pageant Coordinators.

SETTING

The 18th Annual Little Miss All-American Sweetheart Tri-State Pageant, Holiday Inn Hotel and Conference Center, somewhere in the Tri-State area. A "documentary" is being filmed about the pageant and those who are a part of them.

TIME

The Present

ABOUT THE AUTHOR

Mary Lynn Dobson has worked in many facets of the theatre as a director, actor and playwright. Her newest comedy, *Skin Deep* was a winner in the Samuel French Off-Off Broadway Short Play Festival. *Skin Deep* debuted at the Porch Light Production's New Play Festival and was performed and named a winner of both the Shortened Attention Span One-Act Festival and the Frostburg University One-Act Competition. Another one of Mary Lynn's works, *Two on the Aisle, Three in a Van* was performed in the 2009 NYC Fringe Festival garnering the Summer Theatre Citation for Outstanding New Play as well as being awarded Best Ensemble Cast. The play was also honored at the University of Northern Kentucky as a winner of the Y.E.S. New Play Festival and from there went on to receive its professional premiere at the Henlopen Theatre Project. Mary Lynn later returned to NKU where her comedy, *Dracula, the Untold Story* was staged at the NKU Summer Theatre and received its professional debut in a sold out run. She has also penned the family comedy, *The Somewhat True Tale of Robin Hood,* which is published by Dramatic Publishing and has had productions mounted all throughout the US, the UK, Canada, Mexico, Australia and Austria.

AUTHOR'S NOTES

To the directors and actors already aware of the following, I thank you for your time in reading this. I'm including these notes because I've found for the success of the material and those performing it, they are necessary.

I've structured this play to be performed in 30 minutes or less. PACE IS KEY. At the Samuel French Off Off Broadway Festival, the performances ran approximately 28 minutes. The absolute maximum time any performance should last, including all the scene changes, is 35 minutes (and even that's really pushing it). The monologues, especially Brittany's Mom's, should flow quickly. There should be next to no pauses unless it's a specific choice by the actor or director. I have put beats in places, but let me specify for those not used to doing comedy, a beat is not a pause. A beat lasts roughly the duration of a single finger snap. Pauses where an actor feels emotionally connected to a moment are most welcomed. However, too many pauses and dragging out the dialogue will kill the comedy. At no time should the play come to a complete halt and scene changes should flow quickly and smoothly with underscored music if there is not a voiceover.

I have deliberately set the play in the "tri-state" area, which is NY, NJ, and CT. But, do not make the characters sound like the Sopranos. The dialogue should be performed with no discernable accents at all. Also, you are not allowed to change the locale of the pageant. I'm aware that child pageants are most prevalent in the south, but I intentionally did not set the play there. I don't want a theatre, director or actor to spin this into a "zany comedy" that turns the characters into caricatures by portraying them as trashy, ignorant Dixie-chicks. That's not how the material was written, it won't perform well that way and it's insulting to southern women. While this is a comedy, there is an underlying message throughout and playing it "wacky" deadens that. I'm not saying at times some characters don't get a little big and you shouldn't go for a laugh, but the more real and matter-of-fact the material is performed, the stronger and funnier it is. So again— do not use accents and do not change the locale of pageant.

Finally — the prayer at the end is not a joke and the last line is NOT a punchline. Do not play it that way. The last line is not meant to "leave 'em laughing," it's meant to make a point. The prayer and especially the last line should be said with true and complete sincerity by the moms. You will most likely get a laugh from the audience, but it will probably be an awkward one, accompanied by a couple of gasps and at least one uncomfortable, "Oh my God." This is because they don't see it coming. Also, don't be surprised if you get dead silence, and if you do, that's perfectly fine. Just know, laughing or not, at the end of the show if you've left the audience with a slight chill running down their spines, you've done your job.

With love to Dave
who now knows more than he ever wanted to
about spray tans, hair extensions and butt glue.

*(This play is best performed 30 minutes or under. If
you haven't read the Author's Notes, please do so now.*
Setting*: The 18th Annual Little Miss All-American
Sweetheart Tri-State Pageant. A "documentary" is being
filmed about the pageant. As lights dim as we hear some
appropriate "muzak" and the voice of an announcer
booming into the audience.)*

ANNOUNCER. *(V.O.)* Good evening Ladies and Gentleman
and welcome to the 18th Annual Little Miss All-
American Sweetheart Tri-State Pageant. Tonight,
45 of the Tri-State area's most darling all-American
Sweethearts, ages three to sixteen, will compete. But
only one can be, Little Miss All-American Sweetheart
Tri-State. And the winner of this evening's pageant
will go on to Florida to compete in the Little Miss All-
American Sweetheart National Pageant. So hold on to
your seats folks, because there is plenty of excitement
coming your way.

(Lights come up on **BRITTANY'S MOM.** *She is dressed
neatly in something blandly "mom-ish." She is painfully
plain, a bit awkward and has zero self-esteem. She was
the girl who blended into the beige wall all her life. It
wasn't so much she was picked-on, she was just forgotten – and at least when you're picked on, someone knows
you're alive. She will do anything to see to it that her
little girl will never experience that hurt. No one would
question her complete love and devotion for her daughter – it is truly genuine and she does not have a reason
to exist beyond Brittany. She carries a large tote, which
holds beauty pageant necessities. She, as will the rest of
the actors, will speak to the audience who will be "The
Interviewer" throughout the show. At times, the moms
will also talk to their "daughters." When they do, they
will talk either slightly to the left or right. At no time do
the* **MOMS** *touch their daughters.)*

BRITTANY'S MOM. *(Nervous, unsure. Speaks quickly.)* Do I...
do I just stand here? I'm so sorry, I'm not good at
this. Nobody's ever wanted to talk to me before. They
always were interested in Brittany. What? Oh. So I
just talk to the camera? That's it? Just talk? Oh well,
that's easy. *(pause, blank look)* I'm sorry, what do I say?
(listens) Oh, okay. *(beat)* Hi. I'm Brittany Sokowski's
mom and Brittany Sokowski is – my daughter. Brittany
is seven and has been in pageants since she was two.
Brittany excels in pageants. And tonight we're hoping
that Brittany will be crowned Little Miss All-American
Sweetheart Tri-State. Brittany has done really well
in lots of smaller, local, little pageants. She's gotten
honorable mention in, Little Miss Scrumptious,
Miss Ring Around the Rosy, Baby Doll Ballerina Pre-
Junior East Coast, Piscataway Pretty Princess *(especially
proud)*, and she was awarded sixth runner-up in Little
Miss Cranberry Bog. But Little Miss All-American
Sweetheart Tri-State is Brittany's first big, major pageant, with like a big, major money prize, that's cash
– dollars. Brittany *loves* competing in pageants. It's
her life. It's my life, too. But I could never do what
Brittany does. She's so outgoing. I was never outgoing.
And Brittany just loves to be onstage. I would've loved
to have been onstage too, but I never was onstage,
because I'm not outgoing – like Brittany. *(beat)* Anyway,
tonight we expect Brittany to do very well – especially
in the talent competition, which is also called Sassy
Wear. Brittany excels in Sassy Wear. And she's gonna
sing. Brittany's an incredible singer. I could never
sing. Well, I can sing okay, but not like Brittany. Last
year, at our mall, they had a talent search for a touring
company of *Annie*. Brittany got called backed. But she
didn't get the part. I think it was because her voice was,
ya know – too good. *Annie* is full of orphans and they
must've wanted girls that sounded more like they were,
ya know – homeless. Brittany came across too professional. And that's kinda been our problem. Brittany
tends to lose a lot because she does comes across so

professional. I think the judges feel that Brittany's professional-ness gives her a, ya know, advantage. So that's why she doesn't win. *(beat)* Yeah. But that's okay because she'll be always my star. My professional star. *(very excited)* Oh – there she is! *(calls out to* **BRITTANY***, with a big smile waving for her to come over)* Brittany! Brittany! Brittany! Brittany! Brittany, this is the man that's making the movie of you. Can you give him your best pageant smile? *(She looks at the Interviewer, giggles.)* Brittany excels in smiling. Now honey, you go in now and don't forget – be special and sparkle! SPIN!

(She whips out a can of hair spray from her bag and sprays the hell out of **BRITTANY***. Calls after* **BRITTANY** *as she leaves.)*

Brittany! I love you!

(She smiles and waves bye. Looks at the Interviewer with a "deer in headlights" look and. Pause. Awkwardly as lights fade.)

That was Brittany.

(Lights come up on **AMBER'S MOM** *and* **CRISTAL'S MOM** *– pronounced Cris-tahl, as in the extremely expensive, status-symbol champagne [which this woman has never tasted in her life].* **AMBER'S MOM** *wears a tee or sweat shirt that says "AMBER ROCKS" and* **CRISTAL'S MOM** *wears an array of buttons with Cristal's picture. Their thoughts are similar in style.)*

CRISTAL'S MOM. No! No! No! I hate it when you people say that! It's all the media!

AMBER'S MOM. *(overlapping* **CRISTAL'S MOM***'s last line)* Really, you people have to get over this! Beauty pageants don't kill little girls. Maniacs kill little girls.

CRISTAL'S MOM. Child molesters kill little girls.

AMBER'S MOM. Drunk drivers…and gang members – hopped up on crack – with machetes kill little girls.

CRISTAL'S MOM. You have to stop giving pageants AND moms such a bum rap. We're not monsters, ya know. We make huge sacrifices to do this.

(**AMBER'S MOM** *mouths "Huge."*)

You don't want your girl in some crappy pageant. You wanna be in high glitz pageants and *that* costs money for all the essentials...

AMBER'S MOM. Glitz wear.

CRISTAL'S MOM. Photos.

AMBER'S MOM. Swim wear.

CRISTAL'S MOM. Coaching.

AMBER'S MOM. Sports wear.

CRISTAL'S MOM. Waxing.

AMBER'S MOM. Sassy wear.

CRISTAL'S MOM. Spray tanning, hair, make-up.

AMBER'S MOM. *(rubs her hips)* Spanx.

CRISTAL'S MOM. To start, this pageant has a five hundred dollar mandatory entry fee. Then there's a fee for every event you want your kid in.

AMBER'S MOM. Of course the top event is the Ultimate Grand Supreme Queen, but then there's Junior Supreme...Teen Supreme...Mini Supreme...

CRISTAL'S MOM. Swimwear Supreme, *Grand* Swimwear Supreme. Ultimate *Grand* Swimwear Supreme and... there's more, I just can't think of them now.

AMBER'S MOM. And the bigger the event, the bigger the fee. I mean, it's two hundred bucks just to enter Sassy Wear.

CRISTAL'S MOM. And you *have* to enter Sassy Wear cuz the pageant directors told us winning Sassy Wear can get you a modeling contract. But spending the money is totally worth it because the trophies are great and the crowns are a-mazing.

AMBER'S MOM. Oh my God, they're gorgeous. The Supreme Queen crown is like a foot tall. Some pageants have like really nasty crowns. Looks like a piece of crap you got a party store. *(shudders)*

CRISTAL'S MOM. *(emphatically)* But it's not about the crown.

AMBER'S MOM. *(emphatically)* No it's not about the crown at all.

CRISTAL'S MOM. This instills confidence in our girls...

AMBER'S MOM. *(talks to **AMBER**)* What's the matter Amber?

CRISTAL'S MOM. ...It builds their self esteem.

AMBER'S MOM. *(to **AMBER**.)* No, it is *not* scratchy. Why would I spend eight hundred and seventy three dollars on a dress that was scratchy? QUIT PULLING IT! Your neck's gonna get red and the judges'll think you have hives. Wanna go to "nationals" in Florida? Well, scratchy girls don't go to "nationals." Now get out there. *(laughs to Interviewer and **CRISTAL'S MOM**)* Jesus, did you see that? You'd think the child had shingles. God – what girls do to their mothers.

CRISTAL'S MOM. Tell me about it. Last month Cristal almost quit Little Miss Sweet as a Peach because they ruled that no one could wear flippers *(points to her teeth)*. She was totally terrified because she had to compete with her own teeth.

AMBER'S MOM. But you got her through it, right?

CRISTAL'S MOM. Absolutely. *(very proud to the Interviewer)* We placed.

AMBER'S MOM. *(to the Interviewer)* There, ya see? A mother and daughter facing a trauma together, and together getting through it. *That's* what pageants are all about.

CRISTAL'S MOM. Oh! Supreme Hair! I forgot all about Supreme Hair.

AMBER'S MOM. Oh, Supreme Hair's good. That's the one the ugly girls win. Ya see, the thing my husband doesn't get is our money will come back a thousand times when someone sees Amber and gives her that big break. The pageant directors said we could get a reality show out of this. And I say to him, ya hear that? They're the professionals, they should know. But he just keeps bitchin' that we could send her to Harvard with what we spend on these things till finally I say, SHUT UP! After she gets her TV show we'll put the money back into your stupid fund, for ya know, whatever.

CRISTAL'S MOM. Husbands don't get that pageants are an education. Like tonight, Cristal will be fierce. Her motto is, "Keep Your Eye on the Prize!" When she's up there doing her thang, she makes every girl look like a second rate amateur. That's cuz she's a pro and *(listens to Interviewer)* ...Wha? Oh. No. I don't mean Amber's a second rate amateur. *(listens to Interviewer)* Well...sure, Amber has a chance of winning.

*(turns to **AMBER'S MOM** who is giving her an icy look)*

AMBER'S MOM. *(flatly)* A big chance.

CRISTAL'S MOM. *(uncomfortably.)* Sure a big chance. *(to Interviewer)* It's just, ya know, you have to focus on your kid winning. "Keep Your Eye on the Prize" *(to **AMBER'S MOM**)* Right?

AMBER'S MOM. *(to Interviewer. Flatly.)* Yeah.

CRISTAL'S MOM. *(damage control)* And ya know there's another reason why pageants are so wonderful – the bond that we moms form with each other. There is a love, a true sisterhood among us.

*(turns at **AMBER'S MOM** who is giving her an icy look)*

Right?

AMBER'S MOM. *(to Interviewer. Flatly.)* Yeah.

CRISTAL'S MOM. Oh come on, admit it. You want Amber to win more than anything.

AMBER'S MOM. Well, I'd be lying if I said I didn't.

CRISTAL'S MOM. *(to Interviewer)* Look, I want Cristal to win, but she doesn't, I'll truly want for Amber to win. And I know if Amber doesn't win, Amber's mom truly wants for Cristal to win.

*(turns at **AMBER'S MOM** who gives her an icy look)*

Right?

AMBER'S MOM. *(stares at her with no response)*

CRISTAL'S MOM. *(to Interviewer)* So ya see? This is what I'm talking about. *(awkwardly)* The love. The sisterhood.

*(**CRISTAL'S MOM** puts her arm around **AMBER'S MOM** and smiles.)*

That special bond.

AMBER'S MOM. *(Turns slowly to the camera, glaring. Flatly.)* Yeah.

*(To black, lights up on **BRITTANY'S MOM**.)*

BRITTANY'S MOM. *(almost in tears but not whiny)* Ah hi, it's me again, Brittany's Mom? I'm sorry, but as long as you're doing a movie, I thought you might want to know about the not-so-nice side of pageants. It's called jealousy and it's *very* ugly. You see, Brittany has a lisp. And her lisp is a special, God-given quality. It's a quality that spreads joy. You can tell because every time she talks, people start to laugh. And that's why other girls resent her and boy, oh boy, so do their moms! And you know why else they're jealous? Cindy Brady. That show is how old and it's still on television? The pageant directors told me Brittany's lisp could open some important doors for her, on TV like Cindy Brady. And these moms hate that! One mom even told me Cindy Brady did porn. And that's just not true. I did the Google on her. Wednesday Addams did porn, not Cindy Brady. Cindy Brady is an advocate for unweaned kittens and a spokesperson for migraine awareness. She did important things with her lisp and these moms are threatened by that. So what do they do? They take it out on Brittany. Whenever a judge is around, they try to trick her into saying the word, "successful." It's just so mean, not that Brittany sounds bad when she says it because that's cute, it's just they try to trick her and that's mean. One mom said to me, "Why don't you get that fixed?" And I said, Brittany doesn't need fixing! Go fix your own daughter! Start with her name – Penné. That's not a name, that's a noodle. *(beat)* I just thought you should know that. *(sees* **BRITTANY***)* Oh Brittany – oh, no, no, these are happy tears. Happy, happy, happy. Mommy's crying happy tears because she so lucky to have such an awesome daughter like you – and you excel in awesomeness. Now go be special and sparkle. SPIN!

(She whips out a can of hair spray and sprays the hell out of **BRITTANY***. Calls after her.)*

BRITTANY'S MOM. Brittany! I love you!

(to Interviewer, very proud while holding back tears)

That's my Brittany.

(Lights fade to black as we hear one single, drawn out bagpipe note.)

ANNOUNCER. *(V.O.)* Attention please – will the mother of Madison Mullerdow please see the pageant officials. Your daughter's bagpipe has been found.

(Lights up on two pageant directors, dressed in Sears business wear. **ARLENE** *wears a ribbon that says "judge."* **CAROL** *is just a hair-bit savvier the* **ARLENE***. They've both been doing this for years and they are masters at deflecting uncomfortable issues like "questions.")*

CAROL MARIE DITTERMAN. Hello, I'm Carol Marie Ditterman.

ARLENE BECKER-BASS. And I'm Arlene Becker-Bass.

CAROL MARIE DITTERMAN. I'm the director of the Little Miss All-American Sweetheart Pageants and Arlene is one of our most esteemed judges. She has a special gift for picking winners.

ARLENE BECKER-BASS. You're sweet. *(to Interviewer)* As a judge, I have one of the toughest jobs there is, because our pageant attracts the best of the best. And what I look for in a contestant is – an exceptional quality. Something about her that says, *(severely shouts)* "HEY! Look at me! Will ya look at me? Here I am. Look – at – me!"

CAROL MARIE DITTERMAN. *(nodding in agreement)* Not everyone has that.

ARLENE BECKER-BASS. And of course, she also has to be confident, talented, and comfortable in crinoline. *(listens to Interviewer)* Oh no, anyone can enter! Why a mom can walk her baby right out of the maternity ward and on to our stage if she wants. Our only rule is the entry fee must be paid up front, in full.

CAROL MARIE DITTERMAN. And speaking of rules, did you know *(This has been drilled into her by her attorney to cover her ass:)* child pageants such as the Little Miss All-American Sweetheart Pageants are permitted to sanction their own guidelines pertaining to minors as stated in the Fair Labor Standards Act of 1938?

ARLENE BECKER-BASS. *(with a big smile as if she's hearing this for the first time)* I did not know that.

CAROL MARIE DITTERMAN. *(sweet smile as she deflects)* Just a little fun fact off the top of my head anyway on to us – Arlene and I have been involved with this pageant for eighteen years now and... *(She listens to Interviewer.)* I'm sorry, but I'm afraid your question might be inaccurately phrased. The entry fees for the extra events are not money-making devices. The girls are only required to enter one event to participate. The other twenty six categories are purely optional.

ARLENE BECKER-BASS. And all our parents feel that it's well worth it, because – as we tell them all the time, the more events they enter, the more it increases their chance of winning. You know, like the lottery. Now you look like a nice young man, I bet you play the lottery.

CAROL MARIE DITTERMAN. *(sweet smile as she deflects)* She's right, you're cute so you see, entry fees are just like the lottery only more than a dollar. But on to our pageant and all it has to offer. Our pageant awards one of the biggest trophies in the industry, over sixty-three inches tall. It's bigger than the girls.

ARLENE BECKER-BASS. Yes, it's bigger than the girls! And our crowns are superior quality with thirty-three percent real rhinestones. It's the crown every little girl would kill to get.

CAROL MARIE DITTERMAN. *(without missing a beat, emphatically)* But it's not about the crown.

ARLENE BECKER-BASS. *(without missing a beat, emphatically)* No, it's not about the crown.

CAROL MARIE DITTERMAN. It's about being a first-class pageant.

ARLENE BECKER-BASS. Indeed. When you see the lights come up on our stage you'll gasp and say, "HEY! Will ya look at this. *This* is a first class pageant. Look – at – this!"

CAROL MARIE DITTERMAN. And this is a first class, "high glitz" pageant – meaning the girls wear fancy dresses with big hair and make-up and... *(She listens to Interviewer.)* I'm sorry, but we do not feel make-up objectifies our contestants. We feel it enhances their beauty.

ARLENE BECKER-BASS. My goodness, even my minister lets his children wear make-up on Halloween.

CAROL MARIE DITTERMAN. *(to Interviewer with a sweet smile as she deflects)* And what's more wholesome than that? So you see, high glitz pageants are just like Halloween except without the pumpkins. But let's move on to our talent competition. It's called "Sassy Wear." And this is the event every girl wants to be in because... *(She listens to Interviewer.)* I'm sorry, but the entry fee for Sassy Wear wasn't increased because we know the girls will *(does air quotes)* "beg their parents to be in it."

ARLENE BECKER-BASS. Not at all! The fee is higher because it's a showcase for the girls' talent. And all our parents feel it's well worth it, because – as we tell them all the time, Sassy Wear might attract modeling agents.

CAROL MARIE DITTERMAN. The extra charge is a small finder's fee on our part.

ARLENE BECKER-BASS. You know, like a real estate commission.

CAROL MARIE DITTERMAN. *(sweet smile as she deflects)* Exactly. So you see, Sassy Wear is just like real estate except without the acreage. But let's move on to what the event is all about. Arlene...

ARLENE BECKER-BASS. What makes Sassy Wear so fun is that the girls can do any kind of talent routine they want. But be warned – Sassy Wear is not for the weak. As a judge, I don't care if a contestant is three months old, for Sassy Wear, that three month old needs be focused.

She needs to sell it. And if her talent is sucking her binky, then she better be up there saying, "HEY! Look at me. I'm sucking. Look – at – me."

CAROL MARIE DITTERMAN. And while some may feel certain costumes can go over the top, we ensure that everything in Sassy Wear is done in good taste.

ARLENE BECKER-BASS. Why yes, we're well aware some things may not be appropriate for young girls.

(She listens to Interviewer, slightly stumped by the question.)

Well, like…

CAROL MARIE DITTERMAN. *(Beat. Very confident as she saves the day.)* Thongs.

ARLENE BECKER-BASS. *(nods in agreement)* Absolutely. We feel thongs are totally inappropriate for any girl under the age of twelve.

CAROL MARIE DITTERMAN. *(without missing a beat)* Or eighteen.

ARLENE BECKER-BASS. *(without missing a beat)* Or eighteen.

CAROL MARIE DITTERMAN. And we recently did not allow a contestant to participate in Sassy Wear because of the theme she had chosen. It was Destiny Fansler at the Little Miss All-American Sweetheart Prairie Land Pageant. Everyone in her family was a hunter and Destiny had just won grand prize in a youth hunting tournament.

ARLENE BECKER-BASS. She bagged an Elk.

CAROL MARIE DITTERMAN. For her Sassy routine, she wanted to dance with her gun and her elk head. And as cute as that may be, we did not think having a high powered-hunting rifle in a Sassy Wear routine was appropriate.

ARLENE BECKER-BASS. Besides, we felt it gave Destiny an advantage because, well loaded or not, if a five year-old points a semi-automatic at your face and says, "HEY! Look – at – me," you're gonna look.

CAROL MARIE DITTERMAN. *(sweet smile as she deflects)* So you see, a little hair and make-up won't hurt anyone as much as a Single Shot Winchester. But let's move on to tonight – tonight, our lucky winner will take home her crown, trophy and a five hundred dollar *cash* prize.

ARLENE BECKER-BASS. And, we're very excited because we have some pretty generous sponsors. So in addition, our Little Miss All-American Sweetheart Tri-State Ultimate Supreme Queen will also receive *(reads off a card)* dinner for two at the Olive Garden, a rug cleaning from Shag America, a feng shui consultation by spiritualist Henry Wu and a gift certificate for five manicures at You Just Got Nailed.

CAROL MARIE DITTERMAN. Now, does that not say, "First class all the way?"

ARLENE BECKER-BASS. It sure does to me.

CAROL MARIE DITTERMAN. But you know, this is not about the prizes. If you look around, you'll see reigning queens of all ages. And that's what makes this pageant first class. The support and camaraderie of other beauty queens who will not only encourage these young girls to reach for the stars, but who will serve as an inspiration to them as well...

(Lights fade on directors and up on a forty-ish old beauty queen. She's a seasoned pro and is dressed in full-blown pageant grab – crown, banner, hair, make-up and sequin gown which highlights her strategically placed breasts. She holds a small tube of Vaseline in her hand which can remain in her hand the entire time, there can be a stool with an evening bag on it where she can put it down, or if the dress allows she can put it in her cleavage. She looks at "the Interviewer," arms folded in agitation.)

DONNA JANE BRUNELLI-PISSARELLO. No...I'm not Mrs. Poison Beauty. *I'm Mrs. (unfolds her arms, revealing her banner)* POISE and Beauty. I can't believe you just said that. *(opens tube of Vaseline)* And I'm not a Miss, I'm a Mrs. Just because you're married doesn't mean you

can't be a beauty queen. *(listens)* Vaseline. You rub it
on your teeth. *(Rubs a finger full across her teeth. Talks
while she rubs.)* It prevents a sticky smile. *(flashes a smile)*
Believe me, I never go anywhere without *(points to
her head)* my crown, *(points to her mouth)* my Vaseline,
(points to her highly placed breasts) and my duct tape.
(smiles) Isn't it a great crown? I have three armoires in
my living room and one in my bedroom that are just
for my crowns. They all sit on little red velvet pillows
I get custom made by this illegal Chinese lady – *(aside
and very proud of herself)* I got her down to three bucks a
piece. *(catches herself and emphatically)* But it's not about
the crown. It's about being proud of your title. Then
it's about your crown. And by that I mean, when you
win a title, and I've won over hundred, it's your job
to wear your crown. Given, there are two exceptions
– weddings and funerals. I mean, funerals are obvi-
ous because you don't want to be there glittering on
account of... *(laughs a little at the irony)* well, someone's
dead. And you don't wear your crown to a wedding
out of respect for the bride because it is her day...
besides, it's tough enough on the poor thing having a
beauty queen there to begin with, so you don't want to
rub it in. But other than that, you are obligated to *wear
your crown*. And that's what women who have never
been in pageants, don't understand. I mean really,
you should see the looks I get at Marshall's. But you
take it like a pro and remember that you're honoring
your pageant and that's a tough job. Try waving in a
parade for three hours. You're cold, it's raining, you're
wearing a strapless sitting on the back of a convertible,
holding an umbrella *while* waving and God help you
if the nimrod driving hits a pothole – your ass could
end up in front of a Taco Bell. It's not easy, we just
make it look that way. And that's why I'm here tonight.
To be a role model for all these Little Miss contestant
girls. They need to know at an early age how important pageants are. Do you know people hardly even
watch Miss America any more? I mean we're talkin'

Miss America–one of our nation's national institution-als. They say interest has dropped because the ratings haven't been good. And I know why that is — it's this whole "platform" thing. Everybody has a "platform" now. And the bigger the pageant, the worse the "plat-form." Whaa, whaa, cancer, whaa, whaa, AIDS, whaa, whaa that kid on a rice paddy with no school. Look, don't get me wrong, I feel bad about that stuff. But come on people – that's what we have charities for. No one has a problem screaming, "put the care back in health care" or "put the Christ back in Christmas." Well how about put the beauty back in pageants, huh? And I am so sick of the "Hilary Clinton People" saying that being pretty isn't enough because ya know, *(beat, slight smile)* sometimes it is. And I've had three husbands who thought so. I've always been incredibly happy cuz whether I had a husband or a boyfriend, I *always* went out to dinner, they bought me great jewelry and any time they took me on a Carnival Cruise, they upgraded the stateroom. Married or single, I haven't paid for a drink since 1992*. And that's why I'm here tonight – to instill this in these young girls. Not only that, but you never know where positive exposure like this will lead you. I mean, look at me now. I'm taping this pageant for our cable station and you're taping me. So I'm going to be taped while I'm taping. How impressive is that?

(Holds up a finger "wait a minute" to Interviewer, and speaks to the cable person.)

DONNA JANE BRUNELLI-PISSARELLO. *(cont.)* What? *(takes Vaseline and quickly rubs it on her teeth)* Oh Honey, I was born ready. *(to the Interviewer)* Watch this.

(Takes a few steps to Channel 8's camera. She starts off great and though she'll keep going with a smile like a pro, she'll slightly stumble as she realizes she never both-ered to learn the name of the pageant. Beat. Big smile.)

---

* The year can be adjusted to fit actor's age. The character hasn't paid for a drink in 15 years.

DONNA JANE BRUNELLI-PISSARELLO. *(cont.)* Good evening Channel 8, Hackensack! I'm Donna Jane Brunelli-Pisarello, Mrs. *(speaks very deliberately) Poise* – and Beauty. And I'm here to bring you the... Young Miss – Little – Sweet Queen Pageant. *(says sincerely and reverently:)* These little girls are the promise of this great country. They are the Star Spangled Sweethearts here to light the way of our mountain majesty's purple plate of grain. And tonight one lucky little lady will carry home the crown of *(gets a little closer this time)* Young Miss Little – Miss All-America – Girl – Tri-State – U.S.A.!** So don't go away because the magic is about to begin. *(Big smile. Beat. To cable person.)* Good?

(turns to the Interviewer and smiles as if to say, "well?")

What can I say? Just another day at the office. *(pause)* You got a cigarette?

(Lights fade – the voice of the ANNOUNCER is heard.)

ANNOUNCER. *(V.O.)* Attention all contestants – it's only fifteen minutes till the Sassy Wear Competition. So girls, get your sweet little sass on stage.

(Lights up on AMBER'S MOM and CRISTAL'S MOM.)

AMBER'S MOM. *(to AMBER)* No, it is not too tight. Why would I spend a hundred and sixteen fifty on a leotard that was too tight? Oh, you can breathe – are you dead on the floor? *(beat)* Then you're breathing. Amber, I don't want to hear it, go warm up. *(to CRISTAL'S MOM)* I swear I'm gonna kill her.

CRISTAL'S MOM. *(to Interviewer)* But like I was saying, pageants are all about having fun. I have three girls that compete. You know Cristal, then there's Chanel who's three, she just won Little Miss Fancy Pants. And Farrah my baby, has won Beautiful Infant America and Baby *(put her arms up in the air)* So Big U.S.A. Oh! Oh! And

---

** Should an actor want to use this monologue for an audition or competition, they should use the real name of the pageant both times as it may not make sense when the monologue is not done in the full context of the play.

we also have two Bichon Freezes. Their names are Precious and Bouvier. Cristal does her Sassy Wear routine with them in matching outfits and it stops the show. They're such a big part of our family if we had time, we'd show them in dog shows or as Cristal calls them, "Puppy Pageants." *(Pause.)* And we have a boy. *(beat)* His name is Michael. *(beat)* He plays baseball. *(looks at* **AMBER'S MOM** *who nods "yes")* Yeah, it's baseball. And his team was just in a – competition. Well, I know it wasn't a pageant. Duh.

AMBER'S MOM. *(shouts across the room to* **AMBER***)* Amber! – Don't you eat that Jolly Rancher. *(beat)* Because it'll turn your mouth green and the judges'll think you have a disease and girls with diseases don't go to "nationals" in Florida. Now go warm up! *(to Interviewer)* Ya see, this is the part of pageantry that's hard. You have to watch your girl every second cuz one slip-up can cost you the title. We've seen it happen. *(to* **CRISTAL'S MOM***)* Savannah McNair?

CRISTAL'S MOM. *(to Interviewer)* Oh my God.

AMBER'S MOM. Savannah's talent was baking cakes. So she brought in this cake and well, the cake itself was in the shape of a dome and she put half of a Barbie doll on top of it. That way, the part that was the cake, looked like the doll's big hoop skirt. So everything was going fine until Savannah opens her mouth and says, "This is my beauty queen cake and it's my Daddy's favorite because he likes her crown, he likes her banner and he likes to eat her below the waist."

CRISTAL'S MOM. *(to Interviewer)* Could you have died?

AMBER'S MOM. I SO died. But there's your proof.

CRISTAL'S MOM. And that was all Savannah's mom's fault because she didn't have a coach. You wanna win, get the best coach there is. They gotta be chic. They gotta be smart. They gotta be savvy.

AMBER'S MOM. And they gotta be gay.

CRISTAL'S MOM. Now let me say one thing – we're Christians.

(**AMBER'S MOM** *nods "yes."*)

And as Christians we believe that a man should be with a woman. God made our bodies beautiful for men. It says that in the Bible...somewhere.

AMBER'S MOM. And I'm sorry, but I just don't get the whole gay thing.

(**CRISTAL'S MOM** *shakes her head "no."*)

However – the Lord says, hate the sin but love the sinner. So when God tells us we must accept in our lives the talents that He has given these sinners, we listen to the word of our Lord because – well, let's face it, no one can pivot like a gay guy.

CRISTAL'S MOM. Oh! And it really does say in the Bible, "May the beauty of the Lord be upon us" – so there ya go.

AMBER'S MOM. Praise Jesus. *(quickly looks to the left)* AMBER! Don't you drink that chocolate milk... Because it'll give you a mustache and girls with mustaches don't go to "nationals" in Florida unless they're Latino. Are you Latino? Then don't you drink that milk.

BRITTANY'S MOM. *(Enters running. To Interviewer.)* Excuse me...it's me again, Brittany's mom. You wanted to know when Brittany was going to do her song. *(beat)* Brittany's going to do her song. You're going to want to tape it. Brittany excels in singing. Thanks. *(off to* **BRITTANY***)* Oh! Brittany! Wait for Mommy!

(She exits running after **BRITTANY** *spraying hairspray all the way.)*

AMBER'S MOM. *(to Interviewer with a smirk)* Ever heard a little girl with a severe lisp sing a song called, "Be Special and Sparkle?"

CRISTAL'S MOM. *(with a bigger smirk)* It's a treat.

(Lights fade to next scene, we hear the previous pageant muzak and the voice of an announcer booming into the audience.)

ANNOUNCER. *(V.O.)* So let's hear it again for our Little Miss All-American Sweetheart Tri-State, MACKENZIE – ARIEL – WILLAKER! Good night everyone and see you next time!!!

(Lights up on the three MOMS. *BRITTANY'S MOM is frozen, staring at the ground, holding her can of hairspray, nozzle pointed downwards. The other two* MOMS *have none-too-happy expressions, and none-too-happy body languages, perhaps arms folded, a hand on hip, etc. They speak without enthusiasm until they talk about their winnings.)*

AMBER'S MOM. We did well.

CRISTAL'S MOM. We did well, too.

AMBER'S MOM. I'm happy.

CRISTAL'S MOM. We did well so I'm definitely happy.

AMBER'S MOM. And we placed.

CRISTAL'S MOM. We placed, too.

AMBER'S MOM. And you can't ask more than that.

CRISTAL'S MOM. No. No, you can't.

AMBER'S MOM. So we're all happy.

BRITTANY'S MOM. *(staring at the ground without emotion)* Brittany got robbed.

CRISTAL'S MOM. *(comforting her for the sake of the camera)* Oh, come on, she did okay.

AMBER'S MOM. *(comforting her for the sake of the camera)* Yeah, she won Supreme Hair. *(to Interviewer)* Amber won Swimwear Grand Supreme and got fourth runner up.

CRISTAL'S MOM. *(emphasizes the words that will irk* AMBER'S MOM*)* Cristal won *Ultimate* Grand Swimwear Supreme, got *third* runner up and – SHE WON SASSY WEAR!! *(claps)* Everyone LOVED the Paris Hilton theme and when she walked Precious and Bouvier to the end of the runway and said, "That's hot," people went wild. I'm telling ya, between her tan and the dogs, the judges really saw her talent. And you know, *(she takes her time saying this)* the only two things people ever remember at pageants are crowning and Sassy Wear. *(to* AMBER'S MOM*)* Right?

AMBER'S MOM. *(Turns to Interviewer. Flatly.)* Yeah.

BRITTANY'S MOM. *(without emotion)* Brittany excels in Sassy Wear. Brittany got robbed.

AMBER'S MOM. Well, wasn't this Brittany's first glitz pageant? Maybe she needs more experience.

BRITTANY'S MOM. *(coldly, with low growl that gets a bit scarier as she goes along)* No. It's because Brittany's too professional. But one day someone important will see the beauty in Brittany. And it won't be Brittany alone in the parking lot of her prom, sitting on the pavement next to wheel well of the guy that *should have been her date's* Ford Explorer *(tenses up)* listening to him have sex with the captain of the color guard who didn't even notice when she bumped into you *(unconsciously pushes button on hairspray can and sprays downwards)* and made you drop your lunch tray in front of the whole cafeteria! *(throws can behind her on last word)*

AMBER'S MOM. *(Beat. Uncomfortable to the Interviewer.)* Okay.

CRISTAL'S MOM. *(She and **AMBER'S MOM** listen to Interviewer.)* Huh? Are you kidding me? Oh, of course we're coming back.

AMBER'S MOM. Oh God! This is a first-class, high glitz pageant, there is no way we are *NOT* coming back.

CRISTAL'S MOM. Next time, all *three* of my girls will be competing. We're gonna have to get more dogs.

AMBER'S MOM. My husband says I need therapy cuz I'm addicted and I just say to him, SHUT-UP, but I guess he could be right. Seeing your girl all dressed up like a little living doll is kinda like a drug and you just can't ever get enough sequins.

CRISTAL'S MOM. So I hope you get it now. We're not the bad guys. We do all the work and in the end, we want them to win more than they do.

AMBER'S MOM. *(overlapping **CRISTAL'S MOM***'s last line)* And right before you see your girl go on stage, every mom's in the same boat. We're all standing there, more nervous than they are, quietly saying the pageant mom's prayer. *(She listens to Interviewer.)* Seriously? You really you haven't heard it yet?

CRISTAL'S MOM. Get outta here.

BRITTANY'S MOM. Oh, I say it with Brittany all the time. Brittany excels in praying.

AMBER'S MOM. *(to* **CRISTAL** *and* **BRITTANY'S MOMS***).* Come on.

(They hold hands, eyes looking down.)

AMBER'S MOM. Dear God…

BRITTANY'S MOM, CRISTAL'S MOM & AMBER'S MOM. *(slowly)*
Bless our little girl, on this her special night.

Make her confident, secure,

And have no fear or fright.

Let costumes that we pick,

Be styles that will fit her,

(They smile.) Let all her curls stayed curled,

And all her sequins glitter.

And please Lord let her know,

She's our princess everyday,

And one more thing we ask of you,

(They look straight at audience and slowly, in a sincere reverent tone:)

God Bless Jon Benet.

(As the **MOMS** *stare straight at the audience, lights fade to black.)*

(curtain)

NOTE: *this prayer is not a joke and the last line is NOT a punchline. Do not play it as such because it's not meant to "leave 'em laughing," it's meant to make a point. The prayer and especially the last line should be said with true and complete sincerity by the moms. While you'll most likely get some kind of laugh from the audience, it will probably be more of a laugh that's a little uncomfortable, accompanied by a couple of gasps and at least one awkward "Oh my God." Don't be surprised either, if you get dead silence – and if you do, that's perfectly fine. Just know, laughing or not, at the end of the show if you've left the audience with a slight chill running down their spines, you've done your job correctly.*

COSTUMES

BRITTANY'S MOM – Something nondescript – a blouse and pants rather than a skirt or dress. Her clothes can be neat but they have to be drab. Drab blouse, drab pants, drab hair, drab make-up, I think you get it.

AMBER'S MOM – Pants or shorts and a tee or sweat shirt that says AMBER ROCKS. This could also have a picture of "Amber" on it. Colors should be girlie and could also be bright or even neon as long as the lettering can be seen clearly. Glitter, wedge flip-flops are always a nice touch for her.

CRISTAL'S MOM – pants or shorts and a shirt, blouse or sweat shirt. She's the "button mom" and wears an array of buttons of pictures of "Cristal" as well as ones that say: Cristal is SASSY! Proud Pageant Mom. Keep Your Eye on the Prize. Glitz. That's Hot. And *(my personal favorite)* one of Precious and Bouvier, their two Bichons. Because she wears all these buttons, her shirt should not have a print or busy pattern on it as it will make the buttons hard to see and read. The buttons should be two and three inches in diameter to be seen.

NOTE FOR COSTUMING **AMBER'S MOM** and **CRISTAL'S MOM** – Amber's Mom's shirt and Cristal's Mom's buttons should look very "craft store" as if they made them. Amber's Mom's shirt should have iron on letters and the lettering of the shirt and buttons should be clear enough to be read.

CAROL MARIE DITTERMEAN – A pantsuit or coordinates from Sears, JC Penney or Chico's are good choices. Since Carol is the more savvy of the two, her costume should be more understated than Arlene's – earth tones maybe, sensible pumps or shoes. She wears a name tag with the pageant's "logo," her name and her title.

ARLENE BECKER BASS – Like Carol, a pantsuit from Sears or JC Penny, or she could wear a dress as long as it looks like something a woman would wear to a PTA meeting. Her colors can be a little brighter, or she can wear a print scarf to add a little color. She too has a name tag with the pageant's "logo" and her name. However, a ribbon with the word "JUDGE" that is approximately 2 inches wide by 7 inches long, should hang from the bottom of her tag.

DONNA JANE BRUNELLI-PISSARELLO – Full blown pageant garb. Gown, preferably with sequins – more preferably with a lot of them – or, it can be satin in an overdone style. She must have a big ass crown – no negotiation. This cannot be a little skimpy tiara. It should be at least 4 to 5 inches high on her head and have rhinestones. Stalk Ebay – they're out there. Big – done – hair. If it's up, it should be the height of the crown. if it's down, it should be wide. Full pageant make up. She should *almost* look legit, but there should be something about her, her earrings or her make-up or her hair extensions or maybe one sequin too many, that gives her just a hint of tackiness.

PROPS

BRITTANY'S MOM
Can of hairspray

Tissues – optional *(should actress want to wipe her eyes after crying).*

Large tote bag with a picture of "BRITTANY." Contains the hairspray can. For best results, the picture should be a big blow-up of just the head of a very plain looking little girl. It doesn't even doesn't even have to show her hair. The bigger the face, the funnier the effect. No lettering on the tote bag – just "Brittany's" huge face. The tote bag can also have a small portion of a hot-pink or lime-green feather boa hanging out the back end.

DONNA JANE BRUNELLI-PISSARELLO
Small "lip-balm size" tube of Vaseline. She can hold it in her hand the entire time, or there can be a stool with an evening bag on it where she can put it down, or if the dress allows, she can put it in her cleavage.

Microphone – Optional. Used for "taping segment" for Channel 8. If you opt for the stool, it is placed on it. It's not necessary as now most correspondents do not use microphones.

ARLENE BECKER-BASS
Clipboard – Optional. Not necessary, but if you want your actor to hold something, make it a clipboard – perhaps one in a color. Should you choose to use it, Arlene would read the list of prizes off of it.

SOUND

There should be music played during every scene change that does not have a voiceover. All sound should come in almost at the last line of the scene and continue until the lights come up in the next scene. At no time should there be any "dead air." All of the voiceovers should be underscored. Should you want to use an additional voiceover in place of music for a scene change, you may use this:

ANNOUNCER: *(Instrumental muzak such as "Close to You" should underscore this.)* And next, please welcome to the stage contestant number four, Shelby Jane Vilachak. Shelby is five years old and her hobbies include dancing, playing with her puppy, and tornado chasing.

SET

You can perform this piece with no set all. Should you want a set, ideas would be:

A set piece/flat with the design of the "pageant logo" and the name of the pageant in large, perhaps glittering letters. Should be in tacky colors. This would be best placed center stage.

Should you want more than one set, other sets could be the make-up/dressing area with a rack of glitz dresses and/or Sassy Wear costumes and maybe a table and chair with various pageant crap, make-up, tanning stuff, tights, big hair pieces, etc. laying around. An open suitcase full of tu-tus and stuff like that can be on the floor. This set would be used for the moms' scene(s) only.

For the pageant directors' scene, they could stand either right of left of a table with forms etc., and a sign or banner that hangs off the front of the table that has the name and logo of the pageant and the word(s) "registration" or "register here." Or – the table could be the prize table loaded with trophies and crowns, the table sign/banner reads the name of the pageant.

For the Beauty Queen's monologue, a set piece or fly in a sign that says Channel 8 Hackensack. Or – should you have the above trophy table, she could stand in front of that.

PIGSKIN

by Gabriel Jason Dean

PIGSKIN was first produced by The Michener Center for writers at the Lion Theatre at Theatre Row on July 15th, 2010. The performance was directed by Jessie Dean. The cast was as follows:

WILLIAM . . . . .Will Brittain

CHARACTERS

WILLIAM – A high school football player in North Carolina

ABOUT THE AUTHOR

Gabriel Jason Dean has been produced or workshopped at the Hangar Theatre (Ithaca, NY), Theatre Row (NYC), Center Stage (NYC), Aurora Theatre, Dad's Garage Theatre, Actor's Express, Horizon Theatre, the Essential Theatre, Relativity Theatre Concern, Stage Door Players, The Process Theatre, Emory University, Illinois State University, Oglethorpe University and the University of Texas–Austin. His adaptation of *Beowulf* is published by PlayScripts and has been produced in many states and internationally. His play, *Qualities of Starlight* won the 2010 Essential Theatre New Play Prize. In the summer of 2010, Gabriel was a visiting playwriting fellow at the O'Neill Center National Playwriting Conference. His other plays have been a finalist or semi-finalist at the Lark, Seven Devils Conference, Theatre Masters, and the Kennedy Center.

Gabriel is originally from Atlanta and was voted "Favorite Local Playwright" by *Creative Loafing*—Atlanta readers (2009). He was awarded the City of Atlanta Bureau of Cultural Affairs Playwriting Award for his script *Riffed* (2005), the Porter Fleming Prize for Fiction (2003), the Sidney Lanier Prize for Poetry (2001/2002), and won the Horizon Theatre Young Playwright's Festival (2003). Gabriel is currently one of six really lucky people holding a James A. Michener fellowship for playwriting. His poetry, fiction and journalism have been published in *Snake Nation Review, The Tower, Eclectica Magazine, The Melic Review,* and *Creative Loafing.*

Gabriel studied Musical Theatre at Tisch School of the Arts and earned his B.A. with honors in Playwriting from Oglethorpe University. He also studied theatre criticism abroad at the University of Manchester in England. When he was younger and had more energy, he founded and facilitated the Odyssey Program, a drama/creative writing workshop for Morry's Camp, a non-profit camp for underprivileged inner city kids in New York. He is also a co-founder of Relativity Theatre Concern in Atlanta—a new works theatre. Though a non-conformist, he's a joiner: Dramatist's Guild, TCG, Austin ScriptWorks, Playwright's Center. He currently lives in Austin, Texas where— aside from pursuing higher education— he enjoys poorly playing guitar to anyone who'll listen and wrestling with my two VERY large, but loveable mutt dogs, Buster and Argo. His greatest accomplishment to date: convincing his lovely wife, Jessie Dean, to marry him.

You can find out more about Gabriel at www.GabrielJasonDean.com

I. Friday Night

(Lights reveal **WILLIAM**, *naked, holding a football like a fig leaf.)*

WILLIAM. I'm running.

The snap, the turn, in love with my trajectory, the fake, the pocket, the reach...clarity as the ball floats into my grip. The click, the silence in the shell and then too soon, echoing fans in my cavernous helmet like a sea on rocks, churning the sounds of my name, eroding me syllable after syllable.

Bil-ly-boy! Bil-ly-boy! Bil-ly-boy!

The smells of grass and leather quicken the saliva. My heart quakes in the cage – the rapture of predator and prey. I am the hunted, the scent of my base desire, so strong. But something inside me/outside me/around me longs to be taken, smeared into the cold autumn ground, feeling the weight of breathing bodies heaving above me. I'm at war with the North Carolina air, twenty-five yards, and the shame that slows me.

But again, I shuffle unscathed through the bodies of boys and the girls fly high in the twilight, the brass booms and I feign a warm heroic smile. I rest the ball gently on the grass, no antics, and feel the sweat in the arch of my back urging me onward. There's my father in the stands humbly inviting the congratulations.

It's like war, but nobody dies.

My father's words. He speaks of the game in the same sanctimonious tones of his Sunday sermons. *William, you were born to run*, he says, resting his palm on my forehead, the same way he heals the blue-haireds. When I was younger, we'd play two hand touch in the back yard. His only child. His son. My father held my hand in parking lots until I was twelve. And now, he can only lay hands on me in the name of the holy spirit.

Then I was fire, now I am lightning.

II. Saturday Night

WILLIAM. I'm running.

The play of all plays in my mind: shotgun formation, a perfect block, pierce the pocket, buttonhook out, just in bounds, down the field, tasting speed, salty lips, a rush in my fingertips before the ball settles on me and rush of steam, mean, the clock counting down – four, three, two – and the final push, the burn and it's here! I collapse the victor, the prince of 1998, cameras flash, crowds charge the field and I lay prostrate, eyes agape, no words, no words, simply nothing to say.

Saturdays, I run plays on the field at dusk. Tonight, I gaze at the oncoming moon. I peer at my torso in the twilight and wonder how I've not fallen in love with my body before now.

Billy, let's run a couple, I hear Tommy say at the edge of the field. He's quarterback and I'm receiver and sometimes we find each other on the field in the moonlight. He approaches: lean and tall and pimples on his forehead, his shirtless chest the color of the inside of apples.

The half back trick. I shoot through the line, twenty, twenty five and bang, the bullet finds the man.

And then the bubble screen – down-set-hike – two steps, he plants and it spins fiercely into my hands.

You better run, Billy-boy! shouts Tommy, looking like a puppy ready to chase. He knows I'm faster, but can't resist the urge for two hand touch, man to man, and I bolt and he sprints behind me, leaving a spray of turf with his cleats. Midfield, forty, thirty five, he's ten yards behind. I ease and he pushes harder, slamming into the small of my back with his skilled hands and down we go, laughing in the moonlight.

The bareness of our breasts against each other and chill of the mountain air make us understand the meaning of all secrets. I see the devastating fuzz on his upper lip and my face, pulsing, reaches forward and then the click, the silence in the shell. We lay on the grass, pigskin at my hips, feasting in secrecy, the red vinegar moment, and I hear his hands on the ball, the leather making a dull squeak. He bites the cord of my neck and rises, leaving the ball, taut at its laces.

III. Sunday Morning

WILLIAM. I'm running.

Discipline keeps you straight, rigid, lean. Discipline keeps you primed.

My legs sludge through molasses as I run up and down the bleacher steps. The early world is a quiet, painful place. To the top, nearing the press box, imagining State, calves ablaze, in my gut caressing the tender secret of last night's field.

Billy! A shot from a pistol in this silent sanctuary.

Tommy and the offensive line militantly gaze upward. Betrayal pinches my spine.

There's nothing to say. The blitz begins. I could run, easily escape this, but I choose tranquility – or it chooses me – and I understand the click, the silence in the shell; the meaning of fearlessness.

It goes and goes, one after another.

Pussy. Faggot. Cocksucker. Fucking Queer.

My arms, like anvils absorbing the blows. Tommy spits in my face, knees my mouth and cries. I am laughing wildly, alive.

Tommy mounts me, the salty push on leather. Something rips inside. The sound of shame. One smashes my face. I taste my teeth and hear my father's voice.

It's like war, but nobody dies.

Kicks powerfully persuade the air from my lungs. I heave and taste metal.

Oh shit, one says. *He's bleeding!*

The boys break, snapped back to the world, like frenzied dogs suddenly shot sensible with a water hose. Tommy tenderly pulls out and whispers something indecipherable at my face. He scatters and I lay here: ecstatic.

This morning, I heard him rehearsing it – a sermon on abominations. *These people*, he'll say and the amens will roll.

DANCE LESSONS

by Josh Koenigsberg

DANCE LESSONS was produced by Kelcie Beene and At Play Productions, in The Lion Theatre at Theatre Row on July 13, 2010. The performance was directed by Sherri Eden Barber, with choreography by Lyndsay Corbett and Nell Timreck. The cast was as follows:

SUE .... Stefanie Estes
NORM .... Malcolm Madera

CHARACTERS

SUE – Waitress, late 20's. Has recently become scared of everything, but puts on a brave enough face.

NORM – A waiter/delivery boy. No one really knows what to do with him. Has a constant sniffle. Looks creepy enough that people tend to avoid direct eye contact.

PLACE

An empty diner before it opens. Early morning.

ABOUT THE AUTHOR

Josh Koenigsberg's work has been produced/developed at The Public Theater, The Atlantic Theater, Manhattan Theatre Club, 2econd Stage, Ars Nova, Naked Angels, The Old Vic, Center Stage NY, Collective:Unconscious and the 2009 Broadway Pink Campaign at the American Airlines Theater. He is a founding ensemble member of At Play, the resident company for the 24-Hour Plays Off-Broadway, as well as a member of the Old Vic New Voices Network and The Dramatist's Guild. His most recent play, *Al's Business Cards* had an extended run at Theatre Row, was a New York Times "Critic's Pick", and named one of the 10 Best Off-Off Broadway Plays of 2009 by NYTheatre.com. It's published in *Plays and Playwrights 2010,* edited by Martin Denton. He is currently one of the writers-in-residence in The Living Newspaper, as well as one of the staff writers for "Naked Radio" a new radio show produced by Naked Angels Theater Company. Josh holds a M.F.A. in Playwriting from Columbia University and a B.A. in Philosophy and the Arts from Bard College.

(**SUE** *sits at a table in an empty restaurant, in a waitress uniform. She stares past an untouched plate of food in front of her.* **NORM**, *a disturbingly weird looking guy comes in from the kitchen, in a waiter uniform, holding a plate of food. He walks up to* **SUE** *and holds out a peppershaker.*)

NORM. Forgot your pepper.

SUE. Huh?

NORM. Forgot your pepper, I said.

SUE. Um…

NORM. Usually shake pepper on your eggs. Didn't do it today. *(He sniffles.)* Brought the pepper out, so you could do it.

SUE. Oh, I was, um, trying to cut back.

NORM. Cut back from pepper.

SUE. Yeah.

NORM. What for? It ain't salt.

SUE. No, yeah.

NORM. Ain't like it's salt.

SUE. No, I know. It's just…I'd like to cut back, just the same.

(**NORM** *nods. He sits down at another table. He eats. He stops and looks at her.*)

NORM. You okay?

SUE. Huh?

NORM. You okay, I said.

SUE. Who me?

(**NORM** *nods.*)

SUE. Yeah, no, I'm fine.

(**NORM** *eats.*)

SUE. I had a dream is all.

(**NORM** *stops eating.*)

SUE. But I'm fine. Cold out today, huh?

NORM. *(sniffles)* Coat weather.

SUE. Yeah, coat weather. Hat weather too, huh?

NORM. Well, what happened.

SUE. Huh?

NORM. Said you had a dream last night. What happened, I said.

SUE. Oh nothing really. I was just sitting at a table is all.

NORM. Sitting at a table.

SUE. Yeah. It was one of those big black marble tables, y'know?

NORM. *(sniffles)* Oh sure, those.

SUE. Yeah. I was just sitting there. And right in front of me…there was this big glass of milk.

NORM. Big glass of milk.

SUE. Yeah. Just a big glass of milk.

NORM. How big we talking?

SUE. The milk? Oh, about a foot and a half tall?

NORM. Huh. That's big.

SUE. Yeah. And looking at it started getting me real thirsty, y'know? So I picked it up.

NORM. Uh huh.

SUE. And I just started drinking it, like letting it run down my mouth and stuff, getting all over me, and I didn't want to take a breath, I didn't want to stop drinking 'til the whole thing was done with, y'know, but it just wouldn't empty, it just kept on going and going and going, 'til I woke up.

(*They sit in silence for a moment.*)

NORM. Huh. *(sniffles)* Unsettling.

SUE. Well, yeah. Just cause I can't have kids and what not.

NORM. *(beat)* Come again?

SUE. Um, nothing. It's just...I'm unable to have children. So. Symbolism and what not.

(**NORM** *nods.*)

NORM. Sure.

SUE. Um. I shouldn't've said that.

NORM. No, no problem.

SUE. Don't tell anyone.

NORM. Sure.

SUE. Shouldn't've said it I guess. I do that a lot. God. Quick tell me something.

NORM. Tell you something.

SUE. Yeah, so we can even it out. Something about your life, I mean.

NORM. About my life.

SUE. Yeah, quick. Just do it, quick, don't even think about it, just blurt it out quick –

NORM. I take dance lessons.

(**SUE** *stares at him. She makes a "I'm about to laugh but maybe I can hold it in" sound.*)

SUE. What? Oh, wow. Really? No, I mean...Oh God, I'm sorry Norm. *(trying not to laugh)* I'm so sorry!

NORM. Uh huh.

SUE. That was so rude of me!

NORM. No, no problem.

SUE. I didn't mean to...laugh or whatever.

NORM. Sure. No problem.

SUE. *(composing herself)* So, um, like what kind of dance do you take? Is it like Salsa or Tango or something?

NORM. Interpretative Freeform.

(**SUE** *bursts out laughing and accidentally knocks over her glass of water.*)

SUE. Oh my God! Norm, I'm so sorry!

NORM. Uh huh.

(**NORM** *gets on the floor to wipe up the water spill.* **SUE** *covers her face in her hands, still trying not to laugh.*)

SUE. Oh God, it's just I'm picturing you doing it in like this tight little leotard…and your *face! (She controls herself.)* God, I'm sorry.

NORM. No problem.

SUE. Sorry, you must think I'm a horrible person.

(**NORM** *looks up at her.*)

NORM. Think you're wonderful, Sue.

SUE. *(beat)* Oh. Okay. Well um. Thanks. And sorry.

NORM. Sure.

(**NORM** *sits back down at his table. They sit in silence for a moment.*)

SUE. Um. Cold out, huh?

NORM. *(sniffles)* Coat weather. Hat weather.

SUE. Oh right. And glove weather, too.

NORM. Uh huh.

(**NORM** *eats.*)

SUE. Course, I got none.

(**NORM** *stops eating.*)

SUE. Um, gloves.

NORM. Got no gloves.

SUE. Oh you got none either?

NORM. No, I got gloves. You got no gloves.

SUE. Right. Um. Yeah. Got a hat, but no gloves.

NORM. Uh huh.

SUE. I'm sorry – if you're trying to eat –

NORM. No, no problem.

SUE. It's just this dream. I can't shake it from my head, y'know? Like I don't know what it means.

NORM. Sounds like you got it figured out.

SUE. Huh?

NORM. Sounds like you got it figured out, I said. About kids and what not.

SUE. Oh right. Right.

*(**NORM** shakes his head. He shrugs.)*

SUE. It's not really that though. I mean, yes, that's probably what it means. That's what a therapist would say, anyways. About kids and motherhood, and what not. But that's not really why it bothers me. Cause see, there was this long period, where I used to be afraid of everything. Like from when I was seven 'til...well for a long time, I was just scared. Like someone'd say it was time for a bath, I'd get scared I was gonna drown. Or someone'd say it was time to take a car ride, I'd get scared we were gonna crash. And during that time I used to have all these scary dreams, y'know? Where I'd wake up crying in the middle of the night, go running to my Mom. Y'know, "Mommy, mommy, I had a bad dream! I'm scared!" And she'd just look at me and say "Well it ain't like it's life, Sue." Y'know, "it ain't like it's life."

NORM. Uh huh.

SUE. And, y'know – I used to say that to myself so I could feel better. When I'd think of scary things, I'd say, "well it ain't like it's life." Meaning, y'know, "it's all in your head, Sue." And that helped me, cause I stopped thinking of scary things, like drowning and crashing, y'know? But now? Now it's like I see things that are, well...normal I guess. Like I see a really old woman waiting for a bus. Or a man taking off his glasses and rubbing his eyes. Or a kid with a lisp. And it's like suddenly these things are now really scary to me! Like the scary thoughts evolved, like a virus. Like they got immune to all my vaccinations, and now they're stronger than ever. And I try my hardest...I say "it ain't like it's life." But it *is*! It *is* life!

NORM. Uh huh.

SUE. And now I had a dream about drinking milk. No monsters, no bloody death, nothing. Just milk. Just me drinking milk. And it scared the living shit out of me.

NORM. Sure.

SUE. You ever get scared?

NORM. *(sniffles)* Sure.

(She sits down next to him.)

SUE. Yeah? Like what? I mean, what do you keep coming back to, that scares you the most?

NORM. Rejection.

SUE. Yeah.

NORM. Being rejected.

SUE. By women, I guess right?

*(**NORM** shakes his head.)*

NORM. Not really women in general, no.

SUE. You mean like, by humanity and what not?

NORM. Like you stood me up last night.

SUE. Huh?

NORM. Stood me up last night, I said.

SUE. *Me? I* did?

NORM. Well…ain't like we had a date or nothing. Just said we were going out for drinks with some people, after the shift. "Baron's Tavern."

SUE. *(realizing)* Oh my God.

NORM. Went to "Baron's Tavern."

SUE. Oh my God, Norm.

NORM. Closed. No one there.

SUE. Oh my God, Norm, we *were* gonna go there, I swear, but we found out it closed. So we went to that other bar "Sully's" instead. And no one told you! Norm, I'm so sorry.

*(**NORM** nods.)*

NORM. No problem.

SUE. Oh God. And here I am blabbering on about dreams and all this nonsense, and you've been sitting here the whole time waiting to tell me off!

(**NORM** *shakes his head.*)

NORM. Nothing like that.

SUE. No I did! I stood you up! God, I'm so sorry Norm, honestly.

NORM. See, that's what I meant by rejection though.

SUE. I know. God, I'm so sorry, Norm.

NORM. Sort of like what you talked about before. But worse.

SUE. Well sure.

(**NORM** *hits the table.*)

NORM. No. You don't really understand why.

SUE. Um.

NORM. But I'll tell you. *(sniffles)* See, those things you say that make you scared – women waitin' for busses. Boys with lisps. That's me. Hell, I had a lisp growing up. 'Cept it wasn't a lisp. Speech impediment. Couldn't pronounce my R's. Red Rover. Runny Rain. Said 'em with W's instead. Didn't exactly make things easy for me. Then again, had a lot of other problems as well. Can't really hold a conversation for one thing. Always got a runny nose for another. Anyway. *(sniffles)* That sad stuff you see – old ladies waiting for busses. Men who don't stop coughing. That area of life that troubles you when you catch a glimpse of it as you walk on by – that's where I live. And you probably think a guy like me who lives there is used to it. That it don't bother me. That I can stand it. Well I can't. And I try. I try to latch onto someone when they see me there. Try and grab hold of them so they'll pull me out, into their world. But it don't really work that way. Cause that scary sad stuff – I'm covered in it. And it don't wash off. No one wants to bring that stuff into their home. So I take dance classes. Ain't too expensive. Teacher dresses nice. Free snacks, of course.

(A bell rings from the kitchen.)

NORM. *(cont.)* Huh. Order's in. Even though no one's here yet. Delivery I guess. Who would want breakfast delivered, I don't know. Probably some couple lounging in bed together. Who don't gotta be at work. Even though it's a Wednesday.

(NORM *gets up to get the order.)*

SUE. Norm.

(NORM *stops.)*

SUE. Could I…do you think I could see you dance.

NORM. Got a recital coming up, week from Friday.

SUE. I mean now.

NORM. Now? Here?

SUE. Here. Now.

NORM. *(sniffles)* Ain't got the proper shoes.

SUE. Please.

NORM. *(sniffles)* Ain't no music neither.

SUE. Please. I…I need to see something beautiful. Or I might not make it through the day.

NORM. Not very good. Teacher says I got "flat feet."

(The bell rings again.)

SUE. Please, Norm.

(NORM *looks at her. He sniffles. Then with one movement, he unties the knot of his apron and lets it fall to the floor. He slowly squats down, closes his eyes, and breathes in. He comes up, moving very slowly at first, tilting his head around in circles. Then he reaches downward, reaches skyward, goes down, and comes up. He begins to move faster, more fluid. He leaps into the air, spins around, turns over onto a table and spins off it. He slides across the room, leaps over a chair, and spins on the floor. He spins and spins and spins until his body slows down and he stops, going limp. The bell rings again.* **NORM** *gets up and goes to the kitchen. He comes out holding a bag. He puts on his coat and heads for the door.)*

SUE. Norm.

(**NORM** *looks at her. She doesn't know what to say.*)

Um. You got a hat or something?

(**NORM** *shakes his head, shrugs.* **SUE** *goes over to her coat and takes out a big warm hat from her handbag. She goes to* **NORM** *and puts it on his head. She ties it on for him.*)

NORM. Lied before.

SUE. Huh?

NORM. Lied before. About the flat feet. Teacher said I was best in the class.

(**NORM** *tries not to smile. He sniffles. He exits as the lights go out.*)

The End

THE MUD IS THICKER IN MISSISSIPPI

by Dennis A. Allen II

THE MUD IS THICKER IN MISSISSIPPI was produced by Three Monos Ensemble in The Lion Theatre at Theatre Row, on July 17, 2010. The performance was directed by Christopher Burris, casting was by Nedra McClyde. The cast was as follows:

DWIGHT . . . . Walter Simpson III

FAITH. . . . . Jackie Nese

BILLY. . . . . David Spangler

MR. WHITING . . . . Moot Davis

MRS. WHITING . . . . Janelle Lannan

CHARACTERS

DWIGHT – African American Male, mid 20s

FAITH – Overweight, Caucasian Female, early 20s

BILLY – Caucasian Male, 30s

MR. WHITMAN – Caucasian, late 40s

MRS. WHITMAN – Caucasian, late 30s

ABOUT THE AUTHOR

"To realize one's destiny is a person's only real obligation."

New York native Dennis A. Allen II (Playwright) has taken this quote from Paulo Coehlo's, *The Alchemist*, and has made it his mantra. After receiving his BA in Communications, Dennis tried his hand at acting, thinking it would be a hobby, and auditioned for a local repertory company. He landed the role of Moon in a production of Tom Stoppard's, *The Real Inspector Hound* and since that first taste of the stage has played key roles in many plays after, including the lead role in *Beast: A Parable* a one act play by J. Julian Christopher. His love for writing has him pursuing a career as a playwright and Dennis returned to school to get another degree in Theatre Arts. It would be safe to say that he has realized and is fulfilling his obligation. Dennis is a founding member of Three Monos Ensemble.

(Lights up on **DWIGHT** *screaming "Help". Only his head and shoulders are visible, the rest of his body is submerged under mud.* **DWIGHT** *grunts, moans, and screams in a struggle to try and free himself. After a while he stops struggling.)*

DWIGHT. Okay…okay…somebody's going to come. They know you're out here Dwight…they know.

(beat)

Before you left you said, "I'm going for a ride on my bike."…You said it…okay…alright…

(Pause. Laughs.)

This is ridiculous, absolutely ridiculous…I told her, I said, I don't want to visit your family in Mississippi…. It's hot in Mississippi, There are BUGS in Mississippi, I said, and racism and FUCKING MUDDY QUICKSAND… AHHHHH!!!! HELP!! HELP ME!!!

BILLY. *(offstage)* Hush up all that dang noise!

DWIGHT. Who's there? Billy? Billy, is that you? Oh, thank God.

*(***BILLY*** enters holding an open 40oz. Budweiser beer bottle.)*

BILLY. Who's that dere?

DWIGHT. Billy, Billy, over here. It's Dwight. I'm stuck.

BILLY. Dwight? Well, gosh darn Boy, whachu doin' in the mud?

DWIGHT. Billy, please just help me.

BILLY. Guess they don't have mud in New York, huh?

DWIGHT. No, Billy, just concrete and air pollution. Could you please help me out?

BILLY. Where's that fancy bicycle you said you paid…how much you say you paid for that again?

DWIGHT. Billy, please…

BILLY. …Like three thousand dollars for a bicycle. Shit, I paid a hundred for mine and Mama thought I was off my rocker for payin' that…

DWIGHT. BILLY I NEED YOU TO FOCUS…

BILLY. …THREE thousand. Wheww! Where's that bike at?

DWIGHT. It's here in the mud somewhere under me. Billy…

BILLY. Get out?! Well damn boy, you found yourself a serious sink hole. Yeah, the ground ain't been the same ever since, way back since Katrina. The other day John's horse got stuck in some mud, took us damn near eight hours to get 'er out. News came and everything. You ever been on the news?

DWIGHT. Billy, are you drunk? You're drunk. I can't.

BILLY. Don't you worry 'bout my condition there, Dwight. Whatcha needs to worry bout is sinkin' deeper in that mud there. How the hell did you fall in this anyway? They really don't have mud in New York?

DWIGHT. Yes. There is mud. I…

BILLY. …Guess the mud is thicker in Mississippi.

DWIGHT. Would you please help me or at least get someone who can please?

BILLY. Look at you, all polite like. Where were those manners when you decided to date my sister?

DWIGHT. I'm sorry?

BILLY. I said where were your "pleases" when you decided to date my sister?

DWIGHT. Really? You want to do this now?! Are you kidding me?

BILLY. Seems like as good as time as any. You ain't goin' no where now is ya?

(laughs)

DWIGHT. Jesus Christ, would you…

BILLY. HEY, don't you use the Lord's name in vain, Dwight! That there is a sin, Boy. But you like sinnin', don't ya?

DWIGHT. Boy? What…okay, Billy, I really would appreciate it if you helped me out of this. Then we could discuss me dating Faith or whatever it is you would like to discuss. But first please…

(Music plays.)

BILLY. SHHHHHHHH! SHH! You hear that, Dwight?

DWIGHT. Bill…

BILLY. SHHH!! Hush up now. Sounds like music or something. You don't hear that?

DWIGHT. It's my phone.

BILLY. What?

DWIGHT. It's my phone. It's in my pocket.

BILLY. Well damn, Boy, why didn't you call for help?

DWIGHT. I tried to get the phone out of my pocket and then I couldn't get my arm back out of the mud to use it. But thank you so much for that suggestion.

BILLY. Hey, I do what I can.

(BILLY sits on a nearby tree stump. He stares at DWIGHT and starts to chuckle.)

DWIGHT. There is nothing funny about this, Billy. Stop.

BILLY. So you just rode your bike right into the mud. You was just thinkin', "Damn look at that mud let me ride my bike smack dab in the middle."

DWIGHT. It is not funny.

BILLY. Three thousand dollar bicycle!

DWIGHT. Yes. Yes. Three thousand dollars, what is so funny!

BILLY. Three thousand. Shit, for three thousand you would think the bike would have turned itself away from the mud, or screamed out, "Hey Dwight, ya big dummy there's some mud coming, LOOK OUT!"

(BILLY laughs hysterically.)

Three thousand dollar bike shoulda spread wings and flew your dumb ass over the mud.

(**BILLY** *is laughing so hysterically that* **DWIGHT** *can't help but smile.*)

DWIGHT. Okay. Alright. Fine. I admit it was an unwise move on my part to think I could ride through the mud. Could you please just help me out now?

BILLY. No.

DWIGHT. No?

BILLY. Nope.

DWIGHT. Why in God's name not?

BILLY. I don't really like you much, Dwight. Don't like that you're dating my sister. Whole family's upset about it but not for the same reason I don't approve. So, I'll make you a deal.

DWIGHT. Fuck you! You Backwoods Hillbilly Racist Fuck. Get me out of this mud, or I swear to God when I get out I'll have you convicted for attempted murder, and you and your racist buddies can discuss interracial relations while Tyrone buttfucks your Hick Ass!

BILLY. I think you need a timeout.

(**BILLY** *gets up and walks away.*)

DWIGHT. Wait. What?

BILLY. I don't like your tone much there boy, so I'mma go away and let you cool off a while. Might be hard in this sun, but you know what I mean...Me, a racist...shoot, the Parchman family – they racist, the Whitman's... Boy, you have no idea...my "hick ass"...

DWIGHT. Hey! Hey! Come back here! Come back here, God Damnit!

(**DWIGHT** *struggles, moans, grunts and screams. Lights fade and then brighten again to indicate the passing of time.*)

FAITH. *(offstage)* Dwight! Dwight! Where are you?

DWIGHT. Oh, thank God. FAITH! Faith baby, I'm over here! FAITH!

(**FAITH** *enters.*)

FAITH. Dwight? Where are…Oh my Jesus. What in the world? Baby, are you okay?

DWIGHT. Yes, I'm fine. Just stuck. I mean, how long do I have to be missing before it clicks in your head that maybe you should come look for me?

FAITH. You always go for long rides, baby. I didn't…where's your bike?

DWIGHT. It's here under me somewhere.

FAITH. *(laughing)* Oh baby.

DWIGHT. What the fuck is wrong with your family?! This is not funny. I knew I should not have come to this God forsaken place with you. Stop laughing! But you just nagged and nagged and nagged!… "It'll be a nice road trip…You can go and see the Muddy Waters Exhibit at the Delta Blues Museum like you've always wanted… nah, nah nah nah." Take your FAT ASS back to your parents house and get me some help–

(pause)

FAITH. I'm sorry.

DWIGHT. I do not want your apologies. I want you to waddle your ass back through those trees and get me help. Stupid bitch!

FAITH. Why are you so mean to me?

DWIGHT. Oh Fuck me. Really? Really? You want to have a discussion now. What did your country ass eat contaminated dirt growing up?

(pause)

Go. And. Get. Me. Help. Right. NOW!

*(**FAITH** turns to exit.)*

FAITH. No.

DWIGHT. No?

FAITH. Nope. I want to know.

DWIGHT. FAI–

FAITH. …I want to know why you're so mean to me. Why you're always so mean to me. I do everything you want me to do. Every little thing. Two years. Two…

DWIGHT. Faith…

FAITH. I was so infatuated with you, you being so handsome and a college senior and all. And me little ol' freshman new to the city getting the eye of a senior. You were so nice in the beginning. I did your laundry and cleaned your apartment. I even performed fellatio on you. I never performed fellatio on anybody. Not even my high school boyfriend Dwayne Jackson.

DWIGHT. What the fuck are you babbling about? Are you serious right now?!

FAITH. NO! You don't get to yell at me! Not here! Not where I live, where I grew up. Not when you're just a stupid little head poking out of the ground. Yell at me again and I swear, I'll leave you out here overnight.

DWIGHT. Okay. Stop. Stop. I am sorry. It's just I've been stuck in this mud for what feels like hours and mosquitoes have been buzzing in my ears driving me crazy. Not to mention it feels like something in this mud is biting me all over my body. Your brother left me…

FAITH. Billy?

DWIGHT. Please. I'm sorry, baby. I am sorry I yelled. I just really need to get out of here.

FAITH. Okay. I'm sorry, too.

DWIGHT. Okay. Thank you.

(**FAITH** *sits on the tree stump.*)

DWIGHT. Faith? What are you doing?

FAITH. Waiting for my answer.

DWIGHT. What?

FAITH. Why are you so mean to me?

DWIGHT. Can't we talk about this after you get me out?…

FAITH. No. No, because I know that once you're free you won't. It'll just go back to the same.

DWIGHT. Baby, please…

FAITH. NO!

DWIGHT. Fuck!

FAITH. Why are you so mean to me?

DWIGHT. I don't know. I don't know, alright? Maybe I have some deep seeded hatred for women because my mother left my father for another man, or maybe you remind me of this fat bully bitch from elementary that used to beat me up almost every day, or maybe it's my attempt to rectify over 400 years of oppression by fucking and abusing what America finds so precious, or maybe it's the only way I know how to treat you because my father's an abusive prick or maybe just maybe I'm overcompensating because I have a small dick! I don't know! I don't know.

FAITH. You never told me about your mother. Or about that bully. As a matter of fact I don't think you've ever shared anything about your past with me.

DWIGHT. If you do not get me out of this shit right now, I swear to God Faith I will crack your skull wide open.

FAITH. Oh. Okay.

(**FAITH** *gets up and exits.*)

DWIGHT. Wait. Where are you going? Are you going to get help? Faith?! Faith!

(**FAITH** *enters.*)

FAITH. Let me ask you a question, and before you answer I want you to think real hard bout telling the truth, because if you don't tell the truth you might become a permanent part of the scenery of the great state of Mississippi.

(*pause*)

Do you love me?

DWIGHT. Huh? Come on…of course I lov–

FAITH. Have you ever cheated on me?

DWIGHT. What? No. I would never…baby, please. Faith. FAITH!!!

(**FAITH** exits.)

BILLY. (offstage) Who woulda guess it?

(**BILLY** enters)

DWIGHT. Billy…?

BILLY. I always thought that thing about black men having big wee wees was true. I mean why else would my sister be so into black men, ya know? Cause around here that's not the most popular decision a white girl can make. Specially with the parents we got, no sir, not a popular thing at all. Shucks, had our first interracial prom round 'bouts 2008, but people get stuck in their ways, ya know?

DWIGHT. Have you been sitting in the woods all this time listening? You sick, sick–

BILLY. Yes sir, stuck in their ways, kinda like you're stuck in the mud right now. And you could help yourself but you're just too ignorant and stubborn to do so. So what ya do? You do the same thing you've always been doin'. Hootin' and hollerin'. Cussin and carryin' on. Tryin' to use your strength to get out, but the more you try to rely on your strength the more stuck you become. And more you cuss and carry on the more you push those who can help you away.

DWIGHT. Thank you. Thank you very much for your Country Bumpkin words of wisdom. I am forever changed. I've seen the light. Hallelujah! Now get me the fuck out of here. Shit.

BILLY. Nope. I still don't like you.

DWIGHT. Because I'm black? 'Cause I'm a nigger and I'm dating your sister, huh?" I mean come on…

BILLY. NO! I don't like you because my sister tells me everything. Everything. And I've come to the conclusion that you're an asshole. That's why I don't like you. You don't treat my sister good, and you're an asshole.

DWIGHT. I–

BILLY. ASSHOLE! Yes sir, that's what you are. An asshole stuck in the mud, sitting on a three thousand dollar bicycle.

(BILLY *exits.*)

DWIGHT. Wait. Please. I'm sorry…I'm sorry…

(DWIGHT *screams and thrashes his head around.*)

I'm sorry. I'm SORRY YOU STUPID BITCH ARGH!! SHIT. SHIT. YOU FAKE-ASS K.K.K…HELP!!!!! HELP!!!! SOMETHING JUST STUNG ME ON THE BACK OF MY NECK! AHHH! Shit…oh God…help me…please…please…please…

(*Lights fade and then brighten again to indicate the passing of time. Laughter and talking is heard in the distance.* MR. & MRS. WHITMAN *enter, each holding a Budweiser can.*)

DWIGHT. Hello?…Hello?…Faith? Billy?

MR. WHITMAN. Well, looky what we got here.

MRS. WHITMAN. Now don't that beat all.

DWIGHT. Oh thank God. Sir, please I need your help out of this mud.

MR. WHITMAN. Now either I'm drunker than I thought I was, or there's a nigger growing out of the ground!

DWIGHT. Oh shit.

MRS. WHITMAN. Now don't that beat all!

MR. WHITMAN. When the hell did they start growing niggers round here? I mean, shit, I knew they humped and multiplied like rabbits. But a nigger garden? Sommabitch!

MRS. WHITMAN. You think it's some gomment conspiracy to clone Obama?

DWIGHT. Sir. Ma'am. Please…

MR. WHITMAN. I like that. I like it when a nigger calls me sir, but you can call me Massa Whitman. Look at you little jungle bunny growing out the ground! How can Master Whitman help you, little Obama pea pod?

DWIGHT. Please I…

MR. WHITMAN. What, BOY!? You gonna have to SPEAK UP. I don't understand that nigger-bonics.

MRS. WHITMAN. It's ebonics!

MR. WHITMAN. What?

MRS. WHITMAN. Nigger-speak. It's called ebonics.

MR. WHITMAN. Is that right, Boy! Is that what your people call nigger-speak?

DWIGHT. …

MR. WHITMAN. Mrs. Whitman what in God's name is happenin' to our America?

MRS. WHITMAN. Know what I think? I think maybe it ain't Obama, maybe it's the Chinese.

MR. WHITMAN. The chincs?

MRS. WHITMAN. Yea, 'cause they knows niggers are destoryin' America so they created these test tube coon plants to weaken us further. And, and his nigger naps are prolly like spores that travel when the wind blows, and them spores take root near the homes of sexy unexpecting white women, such as myself, and, and those spores grow into Big Black Bucks that break into the home and sexually ravage the unexpecting white women, such as myself… First they puts lead in our beloved toys, and now niggers in our gardens.

(pause)

MR. WHITMAN. The Mrs. is what theys call a conspircist. She sounds a little off sometimes, but I'll be damned if I don't love her for it. She just tickles me to my soul, niggers made in China. Ha! What you call him honey, coonplant? Ha! Yes sir, nothings homegrown in America anymore, it's a downright cryin' shame. That's why me and the Mrs. only drink Budweiser, can't trust all dem other foreign beers. That's why Bud is the King.

DWIGHT. Budweiser's Belgian, you stupid hick.

MR. WHITMAN. What you say, Boy?!

DWIGHT. Nothing, would you just please help me, I have money, I'm extremely well off, and if you get me out I would make sure that you were very well compensated.

MRS. WHITMAN. What, you like a basketball player or something?...

MR. WHITMAN. You tryin to tell me that the King is owned by some goddamn Euro Trash?!

MRS. WHITMAN. Nah, you too short.

MR. WHITMAN. Bud is made by EURO TRASH!!??

MRS. WHITMAN. Now don't that beat all!

DWIGHT. Listen...

MR. WHITMAN. Shut your filthy mouth nigger, shut up unless you wanna die out here. Now you tell me you were lying about Budweiser, and maybe I'll get ya out.

DWIGHT. Ok. Fine. Whatever. I was lying.

MR. WHITMAN. NO NIGGER. You say, "Massa Whitman, I am sorry. I ain't nothin' but a lyin' little coonplant. Budweiser ain't made by no Euro-trash."

DWIGHT. Wha–

MR. WHITMAN. SAY IT!!!

DWIGHT. "Master Whitman, I am sorry. I am nothing but...a lying coonplant. Budweiser is not made by no Euro-trash." There, now I'm begging you, would you please...

MR. WHITMAN. You want some help getting out the mud? Why didn't you say so? Here, lemme water this garden see if I can help the coon plant grow.

(**WHITMAN** *faces* **DWIGHT** *unzips his zipper and urinates on* **DWIGHT**'s *head.*)

MR. WHITMAN. There ya go, Boy! That'll help you grow big and strong. Come on baby let's leave this coon plant to grow in the sunlight.

MRS. WHITMAN. Now, don't that beat all!

(**WHITMANS** *exit. Lights fade and then brighten again to indicate the passing of time.* **DWIGHT** *is visible exhausted and broken. He begins to cry.* **FAITH** *enters.*)

FAITH. Dwight? You okay? I'm sorry I left you out here alone. I...baby, what's wrong? Are you hurt?

DWIGHT. I'm sorry. I'm sorry. Please just get me out of this hole. God. I'm so so sorry. I just never, I...I'll never hurt you again. I swear, I will never hurt you again. I don't mean those mean things I say, I don't, I don't. I don't know why I...Please, just get me out. Those times I hit you and called you names, it wasn't me, I just...I just....

(Music plays.)

FAITH. Shhh! Hush now. Do you hear something?

DWIGHT. What?

FAITH. It's like a faint music.

DWIGHT. Uh...

FAITH. It kinda sounds like...is that your phone? Well, I'll be damned, it gets reception underground? That reminds me. While you were sleeping last night I checked the voicemail on your phone. Heard a message from a Michelle.

DWIGHT. Shit.

FAITH. Oh no, don't look so worried baby, I always knew you were cheating on me. At least I always suspected. You know what you falling in the mud has shown me? Just how small you really are, and I'm not just talking about your wee wee.

DWIGHT. Please...I can't take anymore...You can...call me a coon...a chinese nigger...my face hurts so much...I... just piss on me...I...I feel...

FAITH. What are you babbling on about? Dwight. Dwight? Doesn't feel good, does it?

DWIGHT. Ah...

FAITH. Doesn't feel good being abused by the person you want to save you?

(**DWIGHT** *loses consciousness.*)

FAITH. Don't bother answering. The question was rhetorical.

BILLY. *(offstage)* Hey Sis!?

(**BILLY** *enters carrying a rope and a plank of wood.*)

I called some of the boys, they're on the way. I figured we'd just...shit is he dead?

FAITH. No. Just passed out. Billy I feel really bad. I love him ya know?

BILLY. I know you do Sis, but he needed to be taught a lesson. He'll be fine once he gets a shower and some water in him. Squitoes probably ate his face up good, but that ain't nothing time won't heal.

FAITH. I know. Do you think he'll treat me better?

BILLY. Hard to say, but you should've left him a long time ago...

FAITH. I know. I know, don't you start in on me. Please.

BILLY. Alright. I'm sorry.

FAITH. Billy? Dwight said something funny before he passed out.

BILLY. What?

FAITH. You didn't call him...

(beat)

You didn't pee on him, did you?

BILLY. Faith? What am I, some broke-dick dog?

FAITH. No. Sorry. of course you didn't. He musta been hallucinating. Maybe I should tell the boys to hurry up, he might be worse off than we think.

(**FAITH** *runs off.*)

BILLY. Well, here they come now. Oh good, looks like they got the Whitman's truck, too. We'll have him out of this mud in no time. Him and his three thousand dollar bicycle...What an asshole.

(End of play.)

End

THE BEAR (a tragedy)

by E. J. C. Calvert

THE BEAR (A TRAGEDY) was produced by The New School For Drama, in The Lion Theatre (Theatre Row) on July 17th, 2010. The performance was directed by Mason Beggs. The cast was as follows:

DIANE . . . . Lindsay Brill
EVERETT. . . . . Sean McCormack
FATHER KELLOGG. . . . . Jeremy Ritz

THE BEAR (A TRAGEDY) was produced by Cast & Crew at Washington University in St. Louis in March 2005. The performance was directed by eirdre O'Rourke. The cast was as follows:

DIANE . . . . Lindsay Brill
EVERETT. . . . . .Dan Rubin
FATHER KELLOGG. . . . . Ian Sherman

CHARACTERS

EVERETT FELD, M, 30s or older

DIANE FELD, F, 30s or older

FATHER KELLOG, M, late teens or older

A LIVE BEAR (could be doubled with Father Kellog or done via offstage growling cue or by hiring a circus bear or by slapping a plastic mask on somebody and pushing them out onto the stage)

ABOUT THE AUTHOR

E. J. C. Calvert is from St. Louis, Missouri, currently living in Brooklyn. Recent plays include *Cadaver Synod* (Brecht Forum), *Witness! The Amazing Slipping-Away* (An American Triptych, The Cell), *This One Time I Was Trying to Die: An Exercise in Exposition, Development, and Recapitulation* (The Queens Players), *St. Louis Threw a Party and the Whole World Came* (NSD Theatre). She clearly prefers titles that verge on paragraph-length.

*(**DIANE** and **EVERETT** sit across from each other at the breakfast table in their small home in the Adirondacks.)*

DIANE. You're not eating, Everett. Is it your hormones again? Have you been taking the medication? You have to remember to regulate your hormones.

EVERETT. I was thinking I would go talk to Father Kellog, maybe.

DIANE. Jimmy can't help you, Everett. It's hormones, it's physical. You have to take your pills.

(pause)

Well, Everett?

EVERETT. I think I'm better, already.

DIANE. You went hunting this morning, didn't you? Early. I know, so don't you lie.

EVERETT. ...Yeah.

DIANE. Hunting for what?

EVERETT. I don't know.

DIANE. Hunting for deer? Rabbits? No. No, you weren't. I saw your clothes when you got back – soaked! You'd jumped in that river again, I could tell. You'd been after those salmon. You can't catch salmon, Everett you're a person! You're a human being! You haven't got any claws, you've got – you've got other things instead, fishing poles.

EVERETT. Don't yell at me, Diane. I just...I get antsy.

DIANE. Do you want a divorce, Everett?

EVERETT. No.

DIANE. Okay.

(They stare at each other. He looks at his breakfast and doesn't touch it.)

EVERETT. Diane, I think maybe – I think maybe it isn't the male hormonal fluctuations that have been making me act...like I do.

DIANE. But we agreed that your testosterone levels –

EVERETT. I know, but Diane, that might have been just something I said so you wouldn't worry.

DIANE. It's not your testes?

EVERETT. Well...okay, I'll just cut to the quick of it: it was two weeks ago. I was hunting. Don't yell, Diane. When I was hunkered down near Deer Clearing I saw this black bear – he was sniffing up at some tree, you know, like bears do. And I said, well, who wants a mounted deer's head when they can have a bear rug? And so I shot him.

That first shot didn't do much good, he just turned to me, then after the second shot he started lurching at me, chasing me between oak trees like some kind of crazy bear! I shot him about twelve times all told, and a few more times after he was dead. For safety reasons. And there I was. With this bear. And then I felt all light, and everything got brighter, and then dimmer, and then I could smell all kinds of things, and I wanted to do things – like – like catch salmon and eat honey!

DIANE. You're allergic.

EVERETT. I know, Diane, I know – but I'm saying – that when I killed that bear, I think I got his spirit by accident.

(pause)

DIANE. That's a stupid accident, Everett.

*(***EVERETT** *shrugs.)*

Well, you should have told me earlier. Possession's easy to fix, it's on the TV all the time. You wait here.

(She exits to the garage.)

EVERETT. Where are you going?

Diane!

Diane!

Diane!

(DIANE returns, holding a very large cross. There is a bow on it.)

DIANE. Just help me set this on the table.

EVERETT. How's that thing supposed to help anyone.

DIANE. This is a very holy cross that your son got you for Christmastime, don't disrespect it. I don't care how animalistic you are. I want you to stare at this until you feel faith in your bones and you act like a normal human. That and we might have to start going to church. Are you staring, Everett? Everett, are you concentrating? Everett?

EVERETT. It's nice. It should go in the den.

DIANE. Jesus, Everett! The "den"! Be serious! Jesus!

EVERETT. Don't say "Jesus," honey, not in front of the cross.

DIANE. I'll say whatever I want to! You got some bear god for me to pray to instead? Jesus! Do you want a divorce, Everett?!

EVERETT. I don't – I – no?

DIANE. Fine!

(She clears their plates and begins doing dishes.)

(silence)

Everett, I don't know if I can love you as a bear.

EVERETT. But – but, Diane –

DIANE. Shut up, would you? I'm trying to be serious. I loved you as a person. I don't need you to be all like that, all a bear and all. You were better before. Back then, you'd've never thrown the trash everywhere, or slept outside. You'd've never killed Mrs. Henn's Golden.

EVERETT. Don't bring that up.

DIANE. Why not? You did it.

EVERETT. I wasn't in my right mind.

DIANE. It was still you.

EVERETT. But it wasn't me.

DIANE. Then you lied to me and said it was your testes! I am not doing dishes anymore. I can't believe you, Everett, I thought you knew better than to run around killing innocents, I thought you'd changed since we moved out here! But now you're just a stupid hunter who I'm stupid married to. Jesus! I just wanted a nice quiet life in the Adirondacks. Is that too much to ask you? Stupid! And you have to go hunting! Stupid! You know how I feel about hunting.

EVERETT. I didn't want to bring it up. I'm just trying to be honest with you, because you're my soulmate and we need to have an honest loving relationship.

DIANE. Have you been reading my Dr. Romance Relationship books?

EVERETT. ...No?

DIANE. Jesus, Everett, you're a hunter, a bear, and now you're a queer, too.

EVERETT. Diane, don't. My brother's a queer.

DIANE. Everett, I love you. But you can't stay like this. You have to do something.

EVERETT. It's weird.

DIANE. I know it's weird, Everett, everything is weird, and people still do things!

EVERETT. I know.

DIANE. So do something!

EVERETT. What?

DIANE. I don't care! Do something! Do something! Do something!

(She hits him with her breakfast banana and he jumps up, growling.)

...Everett.

*(**EVERETT** lets out a feral growl and jumps up on the table. He rears up to his full height, baring his teeth. **DIANE** cowers.)*

Stop it, Everett! Stop it! Stop it! You're being a bear!

(He crosses to her. She plays dead. He paws her body around, but she remains still. He lets out a final resounding roar and runs out the patio door on all fours. DIANE remains still.)

(There is a knock at the front door.)

DIANE. *(cont.)* It's not a good time.

FATHER KELLOG. Then it's a good thing I'm here, Mrs. Feld.

DIANE. Oh, let yourself in, Jimmy.

FATHER KELLOG. Um…where's…what happened?

DIANE. Nothing, nothing.

*(***FATHER KELLOG*** *touches the cross.)*

FATHER KELLOG. Ooh – I love this one! It's fancy, you can tell from the size.

DIANE. Oh – yes. We were thinking of putting it in the den. A gift from our Jimmy-pie!

FATHER KELLOG. Mom, look, I'm a priest now, and I wish you'd treat me with respect for that authority, okay?

DIANE. You know I respect you, pumpkin.

FATHER KELLOG. "Father Kellog."

DIANE. You really want me to call you that? When it's just us?

FATHER KELLOG. It's who I am now.

DIANE. I don't see why you couldn't just be Father Feld.

FATHER KELLOG. I had to cut all ties, Mom! Don't you know anything? No offense, Mom, no offense, it's just the way of the Lord. Okay?

DIANE. Okay. Would you like some – uh – coffee?

FATHER KELLOG. What happened here? Did Mr. Feld do this?

DIANE. No, no. Well, yes. He's not himself.

FATHER KELLOG. He's been drinking.

DIANE. No, it's just that, well, he's – kind of a bear right now.

FATHER KELLOG. He should still be able to control his temper, no matter what mood he's in. Control is vital. Control is what sets the humans, God's own image, apart from the beasts.

DIANE. No, I mean, really a bear. Says he's possessed.

FATHER KELLOG. Demons!

DIANE. A bear. A bear-ghost. A bear's spirit.

FATHER KELLOG. That's silly.

DIANE. I know, it's ridiculous, but Jimmy –

FATHER KELLOG. Ah –

DIANE. Father Kellog.

FATHER KELLOG. Thank you. So, Mrs. Feld – where's Dad?

DIANE. In the forest. This bear spirit is not good for his health. If he'd only told me what was wrong before, I could've gotten him help. He'd been eating a lot, for the coming hibernation season I suppose. He doesn't realize that he can't hibernate, he's a working man. He's got responsibilities. And think of the calories. Stubborn man won't think of anything, not even for a second. I could accept him as a bear, Jimmy, if only he'd act like a decent human being.

FATHER KELLOG. Well, Mrs. Feld, I'd be willing to try an exorcism.

DIANE. Oh, Jimmy –

FATHER KELLOG. I am a priest and when I see a man possessed –

DIANE. Jimmy, we stopped going to church when you were born.

FATHER KELLOG. It's all the same under the eyes of the Lord. Don't you worry, Mrs. Feld, we'll free your husband from the devil's grasp in no time at all. Just wait here, I'll get a few things from my bike. Mrs. Feld – if he gets back before I do, don't be afraid. Demons can smell fear. It makes them grow stronger. Don't let him know you're afraid, or who knows what kind of damage a being like that could do.

I love you, Mom.

(He rushes out the front door. **EVERETT** *immediately enters through the back door.)*

EVERETT. Honey?

*(***DIANE*** *screams.)*

It's just me, I'm sorry. I got control of myself, just had to blow off some steam.

*(***DIANE*** *brandishes a frying pan.)*

DIANE. You stay right where you are! I am not afraid!

EVERETT. Honey, it's just me. Everett.

DIANE. Don't move! Jimmy will be back and he'll take care of you!

EVERETT. Jimmy?

*(***FATHER KELLOG*** *enters, carrying a water bottle, rosary beads, and a Bible.)*

FATHER KELLOG. Back, demon!

(He squirts the bottle at **EVERETT.***)*

EVERETT. Hey.

DIANE. It didn't work!

FATHER KELLOG. I haven't blessed it yet.

DIANE. You hurry, I'll hold him back –

EVERETT. You guys –

DIANE. Back, demon! Back!

EVERETT. Diane, it's me.

DIANE. It knows my name!

FATHER KELLOG. Mr. Feld is still in there somewhere, ma'am, that's why we can't just kill it.

EVERETT. Whoa, whoa – would you hold on? It's me. Everett Cannon Feld, husband and father. You know me. Just take a second to look at me and realize what you're doing.

*(***FATHER KELLOG*** *squirts him in the face with the water bottle, then smacks him with the rosary beads and the Bible.)*

DIANE. Wait –

> *(**FATHER KELLOG** continues squirting and smacking and chanting for the bear demons to leave.)*

Father Kellog – Father Kellog! Jimmy!

EVERETT. Stop it!

DIANE. Jimmy, you stop hitting your father.

EVERETT. Ow! Jesus!

FATHER KELLOG. But he's possessed.

EVERETT. I'm okay, Jimmy.

DIANE. Look at him, Jimmy, he looks fine to me.

FATHER KELLOG. You're making the worst mistake of your life.

DIANE. Don't say that.

FATHER KELLOG. *(to **EVERETT**)* I know it's you I'm staring at, demon. And I won't forget about you, either. Don't think I'll just let you live. Not like this. You'd have to kill me first.

> *(**FATHER KELLOG** backs toward the door.)*

DIANE. You leaving so soon, Jimmy?

FATHER KELLOG. I have to phone the Vatican. I'll be praying for your souls. I only hope you are able to do the same!

> *(**FATHER KELLOG** exits.)*

DIANE. Jimmy, do not say things like that to your parents.

EVERETT. *(growling)* We raised you, you parent-beating little brat!

> *(**EVERETT** lurches out the front door, bear style. **DIANE** runs to the window.)*

DIANE. EVERETT! NO!

> *(Outside, **FATHER KELLOG** shrieks, ringing his bicycle bell for help as he is chased around the yard by his father. **EVERETT** catches him, mauls him, and lets out a resounding, triumphant roar.)*

Don't chew him, Everett.

(**EVERETT**, *returning to humanity, comes to the front door to find it locked behind him. He knocks.*)

DIANE. *(cont.)* Screw you!

EVERETT. Let me in, Diane.

DIANE. You just mauled our son to death!

EVERETT. I didn't mean to. The bear –

DIANE. You shut up about the bear!

EVERETT. In bear culture, infanticide is practically acceptable –

DIANE. This isn't "bear culture," Everett! This is the Adirondacks, this is America!

EVERETT. I'm sorry, honey.

DIANE. You just sleep outside tonight. I thought you'd changed, Everett.

EVERETT. I did.

DIANE. Sure, and then you went right back.

EVERETT. It was an accident.

DIANE. Is everything an accident with you? Take responsibility for once.

(The door opens.)

Hey!

EVERETT. Key was under the mat.

DIANE. Well. I'm going to my sister's house.

EVERETT. Are you...are you leaving me? Diane?

DIANE. You had your chance. And you used it to disembowel our son.

(She goes to the bedroom to pack.)

EVERETT. It's not my fault I'm easily possessed!

Diane!

Diane!

Diane!

(**DIANE** *re-enters with a small suitcase.*)

You're not really leaving.

DIANE. Goodbye, Everett.

EVERETT. But – but – look, I'm cleaning the kitchen.

DIANE. That will be nice for you. Goodbye.

EVERETT. I could rip you apart!

DIANE. Shut up, Everett.

(**DIANE** *exits.*)

EVERETT. Well – yeah?

BEARS DON'T MATE FOR LIFE ANYHOW!

God.

(*pause*)

Hey, you can come in.

(*A full-grown male bear swaggers into the room.*)

Yeah, have a seat wherever. My wife's out. I don't know for how long, but you know, whatever. Freedom, you know? Yeah.

…You want a beer or something?

End of Play

OFF-OFF-BROADWAY FESTIVAL PLAYS

THIRTEENTH SERIES

Beached   A Grave Encounter   No Problem   Reservations for Two
Strawberry Preserves   What's a Girl to Do

FOURTEENTH SERIES

A Blind Date with Mary   Bums   Civilization and Its Malcontents   Do Over
Tradition 1A

FIFTEENTH SERIES

The Adventures of Captain Neato-Man   A Chance Meeting Chateau Rene
Does This Woman Have a Name?   For Anne   The Heartbreak Tour
The Pledge

SIXTEENTH SERIES

As Angels Watch   Autumn Leaves   Goods   King of the Pekinese Yellowtail
Uranium   Way Deep   The Whole Truth   The Winning Number

SEVENTEENTH SERIES

Correct Address   Cowboys, Indians and Waitresses   Homebound   The Road
to Nineveh   Your Life Is a Feature Film

EIGHTEENTH SERIES

How Many to Tango?   Just Thinking   Last Exit Before Toll   Pasquini the
Magnificent   Peace in Our Time   The Power and the Glory
Something Rotten in Denmark   Visiting Oliver

NINETEENTH SERIES

Awkward Silence   Cherry Blend with Vanilla   Family Names   Highwire
Nothing in Common   Pizza: A Love Story   The Spelling Bee

TWENTIETH SERIES

Pavane   The Art of Dating   Snow Stars   Life Comes to the Old Maid   The
Appointment   A Winter Reunion

TWENTY-FIRST SERIES

Whoppers   Dolorosa Sanchez   At Land's End   In with Alma
With or Without You   Murmurs   Ballycastle

TWENTY-SECOND SERIES

Brothers   This Is How It Is   Because I Wanted to Say Tremulous   The Last
Dance   For Tiger Lilies Out of Season   The Most Perfect Day

OFF-OFF-BROADWAY
FESTIVAL PLAYS

TWENTY-THIRD SERIES

The Way to Miami   Harriet Tubman Visits a Therapist   Meridan, Mississippi
Studio Portrait   It's Okay, Honey   Francis Brick Needs No Introduction

TWENTY-FOURTH SERIES

The Last Cigarette   Flight of Fancy   Physical Therapy   Nothing in the World Like It
The Price You Pay   Pearls Ophelia   A Significant Betrayal

TWENTY-FIFTH SERIES

Strawberry Fields   Sin Inch Adjustable   Evening Education   Hot Rot
A Pink Cadillac Nightmare   East of the Sun and West of the Moon

TWENTY-SIXTH SERIES

Tickets, Please!   Someplace Warm   The Test   A Closer Look
A Peace Replaced   Three Tables

TWENTY-SEVENTH SERIES

Born to Be Blue   The Parrot   Flights   A Doctor's Visit
Three Questions   The Devil's Parole

TWENTY-EIGHTH SERIES

Along for the Ride   A Low-Lying Fog   Blueberry Waltz   The Ferry
Leaving Tangier   Quick & Dirty (A Subway Fantasy)

TWENTY-NINTH SERIES

All in Little Pieces   The Casseroles of Far Rockaway   Feet of Clay
The King and the Condemned   My Wife's Coat   The Theodore Roosevelt Rotunda

THIRTIETH SERIES

Defacing Michael Jackson   The Ex   Kerry and Angie   Outside the Box
Picture Perfect   The Sweet Room

THIRTY-FIRST SERIES

Le Supermarché   Libretto   Play #3   Sick   Pischer   Relationtrip

THIRTY-SECOND SERIES

Opening   Circuit Breakers   Bright. Apple. Crush.
The Roosevelt Cousins, Thoroughly Sauced   Every Man   The Good Book

THIRTY-THIRD SERIES

F*cking Art   Ayravana Flies or A Pretty Dish   The Thread Men
The Dying Breed   The Grave   Juniper; Jubilee

THIRTY-FOURTH SERIES

Drop   The Education of Macoloco   realer than that
The Student   Thucydides   Just Knots

SAMUELFRENCH.COM

OTHER TITLES AVAILABLE FROM SAMUEL FRENCH

ACCIDENTS HAPPEN
J. Michael DeAngelis, Pete Barry & John P. Dowgin

Collection of short plays / Comedy

Winner! 2009 NJACT Perry Award for Outstanding Production of an Original Play

Seven of The Porch Room's best short plays collected together into an evening of comedy that proves that no matter what you plan for - accidents happen.

Shorts include:

Accidents Happen - Please beware of all safety procedures and take note of the emergency exits.

Nine Point Eight Meters Per Second Per Second - Balthazar Kent, ejected from an airplane, tries to regain control of his life through his cellphone.

Reunion Special - A desperate former child actor reunites with his now adult co-stars at a funeral.

The Clive Way - A motivational speaker mistakenly tries to empower a group of newly rehabilitated anger-management patients.

Hangman - A budding teenage philosopher-scientist searches for the truth by experimenting on his friend with a hallucinogenic cocktail.

Tricks of the Trade - Ralph teaches Eddie how to sell your soul for success.

The Banderscott - An infomercial marketer is pitched an astonishing product.

CHRISTMAS SHORTS
Matt Hoverman

Collection of short plays / Holiday Comedy

A celebrated Winner of the 2009 Samuel French Off Off Broadway Short Play Festival, playwright Matt Hoverman brings an evening of hilarious short holiday comedies to the stage. A wonderful alternative for theatres tired of mounting the traditional seasonal play, *Christmas Shorts* offers five original plays that humorously comment on holiday themes: family, the nativity, Xmas cards, and elves. An outstanding Christmas collection for any theatre!

Included are the plays: *Going Home, The Christmas Witch, Xmas Cards, Nativity,* and the Samuel French Festival award-winning play *The Student.*

www.ingramcontent.com/pod-product-compliance
Lightning Source LLC
Chambersburg PA
CBHW070625120726
47909CB00004B/1323